The Shape-Changer's Wife

The Shape-Changer's Wife

Sharon Shinn

ACE BOOKS, NEW YORK

For my mother

For my mother

The Shape-Changer's Wife

One

UNTIL AUBREY ARRIVED IN THE VILLAGE TO STUDY WITH Glyrenden, he had no idea that the great wizard had taken a wife. At the time, drinking an ale in the warm, lightless tavern which was situated at the very center of town (in fact, the heart of the small community), he did not think it mattered one way or the other. Nonetheless, he was surprised. From what old Cyril had told him, Glyrenden did not seem like the kind of man disposed toward the softer passions. But then, it was obvious Cyril did not like the court magician, and perhaps his unflattering words could be traced to professional jealousy.

It had not been Aubrey's idea to apprentice with the shape-changer. He had been certain Cyril could teach him what he wanted to know, for Cyril was renowned in this land and three lands farther west as the greatest wizard in seven generations. But Cyril, who had willingly and with patient generosity shared with him the spells and knowledge it had taken him eighty years to accumulate, flatly refused to instruct him in the matters of transmogrification.

"But why not?" Aubrey had asked him, a dozen times, a hundred times. "You know the spells. You have cast them."

1

"They are barbaric spells," Cyril had said, and would say no more. But Cyril's conscience had troubled him. Alchemy of every sort was essential to the education of any well-rounded wizard, and Aubrey was, even this young, showing signs of being among the most gifted wizards of this century. So he wrote to Glyrenden and proposed Aubrey as a student; and Glyrenden wrote back to accept the charge. Cyril had sent Aubrey on his way with the briefest words of advice.

"Learn everything he teaches you so well you can cast his own spells back at him," the old wizard had said. "Glyrenden respects only those stronger than he is, and those he hates. If you cannot beat him, he will destroy you. Already you are a better magician than he in many of the branches, but if he sees he can best you in this one branch, he will use his skill against you. So you must learn everything, and forget nothing, and beware of Glyrenden at all times."

"You alarm me," Aubrey said mildly, smiling. He was a fair-haired, open-faced, sunny-tempered young man who had a fearsome passion for knowledge and an absolute faith in his own abilities. He had never yet come across something he could not do; but this easy ability did not make him arrogant or malicious. Rather, it turned him benevolent and charming, happy with himself and his world. "Why do you send me to him, if he is so menacing?"

"It would not do you much harm to face a challenge at this point in your career," Cyril muttered.

Aubrey laughed. "And why has he agreed to tutor me if he is such an Ogre? He does not sound like the type to gladly accept troublesome pupils."

Cyril gave him a quick sideways look from his narrow blue eyes, the glancing look like sunlight glittering across water, a look that gave away more than the spoken answer if Aubrey could only read it. "Because he cannot conceive that you will prove to be better than he, and he wants a chance to prove it."

Aubrey gave it up. "I had best be on my guard during my whole stay at his house, then," he said.

"Yes," said Cyril. "I think you had better."

So Aubrey had packed up his thin saddlebags and tossed his threadbare green cloak over his shoulders, and walked the three hundred miles to the wizard's house when he could not beg the odd ride from the peddlers and merchants that traveled the North King's Road. He had arrived late one evening and elected to sleep overnight at the town's single hostel before presenting himself at Glyrenden's door. And in the morning, there was the fair to see, and the pretty girls to flirt with, and flowers to buy for some of them in the market; so it was afternoon before he was ready to start on the final mile of his journey.

He had fortified himself with a glass of ale at the tavern, and it was then he learned that Glyrenden had a wife. Aubrey had made friends with the tavernkeeper over his lunch of bread and cheese, and had told the man what he could remember about the condition of the roads between there and Southport. And then he had asked the man for directions to the home of Glyrenden, and he had seen the strangest look cross the fellow's tanned and honest face.

"On the way there, are you," the man had said, and his voice became flat and distant, the voice of a man talking to a customer to whom he must be civil and not to a man he liked. "Well, you takes this road here, that runs outside me door, and follows it to where it forks left. After that, you'll see three crossroads, and at each you takes the left cross. And when you comes to his house, you'll know it."

Aubrey gave the man his easy smile. "Veering to the sinister," he said. "That seems to fit. It should be simple to remember."

The man's dark eyes gave back no hint of a smile, no hint that he had even comprehended the small joke. "Will you be leaving soon?" he asked politely.

"As soon as my drink is done. Tell me, does Glyrenden come to town often? Or does he move only between his place and the king's castle?"

"He comes," the barkeeper said coolly, "but not often. She comes even less."

"She?"

The man lifted his hands involuntarily from the rubbed-wood counter, then deliberately set them down again. Aubrey wondered what gesture he had been going to make; the man's whole body was stiff with distaste. "The wizard's wife."

"He's married?"

"Aye. Or at least, the woman has lived there any time these three years now."

"Cyril didn't tell me that."

"Pardon, sir?"

"Nothing. Nothing at all." Aubrey smiled again, laid a gold piece on the counter, and smiled privately once more to see the expression with which the barkeeper regarded the coin. Glyrenden was not much liked in this place, it seemed, and those who trafficked with him fell instantly under the same suspicion. "I hope I will see you again," he added pleasantly. "This is the closest village, so I understand, to Glyrenden's place."

"Aye," the man said somewhat dryly. "It is that."

"Then no doubt I will be down now and then when I am thirsty for a drop or two."

"Of course. We'll be looking to see you again, sir," the tavernkeeper said.

Aubrey grinned. "Well, good. Till then, my man."

"Till then."

The walk through the village and up through the forested foothills was a pretty one, the afternoon being cool for summer, and the slanting sun giving to all the late-green trees a luxuriant glow. Aubrey hummed as he walked, and now and then broke out into actual song, and he strode along at a brisk, healthy pace and laughed at his own youth and eagerness. Neither Cyril's dour warnings nor the tavernkeeper's hostility sobered him. It was a fine day and he was in a fine mood and on his way to a place he had never been, to acquire a knowledge he had long coveted; and he could not imagine a time when the world had seemed any better or full of more promise.

As the villager had told him, the house of Glyrenden was impossible to miss. It was separated from the main path by an overgrown track scarcely wide enough to admit a cart to pass, and it was huge: three stories of iron-gray rock piled together in a careless fashion. It was somberly accented at the front entrance and at widely spaced intervals with panels of dark wood which served as doors and window shutters. Dead ivy striped the southernmost turret, and live ivy curled possessively around every other lintel, threshold and outthrust brick. An untended garden ran wild in a border five feet deep as far around the dwelling as Aubrey could see—roses twining with the ivy up the walls, yellow sunflowers heavy with the weight of their powdery brown hearts, hollyhocks opening their lush and vulgar blossoms to catch the last rays of the setting sun. The only sound was that of Aubrey's boots crunching across the gravel, and the bend and sigh of the low-hanging branches and bushes that he pushed aside as he struggled up the path to the house.

When he knocked, his fist created such a small sound against the heavy wood of the door, he doubted it could be heard by anyone inside those tumbled walls. He knocked again three times before he noticed the rusty chain hanging to one side of the door; then he crossed the porch to pull that vigorously. Distantly, he heard the clamor of warning bells inside the fortress and was satisfied that someone would now be alerted to his presence. He hammered on the wood one more time just in case.

He waited, but there was no response. Impatiently, he stepped off the low, cracked stone porch to look up at what he could see of the face of the building: a few closed windows, and the fluttering ivy. From where he stood, it was impossible to tell if there was any smoke drifting up from the back kitchens or the front parlors, and he had not bothered to look for any as he cleared his way up the front walk. Perhaps no one was home. He stepped back on the porch again and gave the bell chain another hearty pull.

On the instant, the door opened. Aubrey turned quickly toward the sound, his ready smile back on his face. A tall woman stood framed in the doorway, holding the door open with both hands as though it were heavy. Her hair, braided in a coronet around her head, was as dark as the wood of the door, her gown was as gray as the stone, and her eyes were a green so rich they were a startling source of color in this drab place. On her face was an expression of utter indifference.

"What do you want?" she asked. She sounded neither friendly nor unfriendly; she did not even sound curious.

Some of Aubrey's smile had faded to be replaced by a quizzical look. "Hello," he said, starting with his mildest grade of charm. "I am Aubrey. I was sent here by the magician Cyril of Southport to study with Glyrenden. I believe he is expecting me."

"Is he?" the woman asked. "I didn't know."

Aubrey waited a moment, but that seemed to be all she had to say. He turned his charm a fraction of a degree higher. "Perhaps he has forgotten," he said. "Is he here? May I come in and speak with him?"

She was still holding the door with both hands, but not as though she minded the weight. For a moment, Aubrey thought she would refuse; then she shrugged, and pulled the door wider. He stepped inside. "He's not here," she said, as he crossed the threshold. "He ought to be back tomorrow or the next day, though."

Aubrey was looking around him in some astonishment, and so at first did not catch the import of her words. The neglect of the outer grounds had led him to expect some deterioration inside as well, but from what he could see of the front hallway and parlor, the house was in utter disarray. Dust lay inches thick on every surface; his boots had sunk in a pile of it, and the woman's tracks could be plainly seen in this corridor which she had traversed to answer the door. Cobwebs competed with cut glass as the most conspicuous feature of the handsome chandelier hanging over their heads; the iron suit of armor that guarded a niche down the hall was beginning to rust over. A pervasive odor that seemed to rise from the gray bricks themselves was compounded half of dampness and half of dust.

He could not keep the amazement off his face when

he turned to look at the woman who had let him in. Her eyes traveled where his had wandered, to see what had caused him to look so. "It is not so bad in the rooms where we mostly live," she remarked, seemingly unembarrassed. "Arachne does what she can, but the place is too big. No one ever uses this part of the house, anyway."

It was then that he remembered what she had said when he first stepped inside. "You say Glyrenden is not here?" he repeated. "Is it inconvenient that I stay, then?"

Her eyes came back to him and noticed his travel-stained clothes and the saddlebags he carried over his shoulder. "Oh," she said. "You were planning to live with us, I take it?"

He felt suddenly awkward and foolish, both rare things for him. "Well, as Glyrenden's pupil—but, after all, it is not far from the village, and I can just as easily return each day—and if he is not here—"

What may have been a smile brushed across her mouth and was gone. "Do not trouble yourself over appearances," she said. "There are servants here. Of a sort. And none of the villagers is likely to accuse me of entertaining a lover, even if they spoke to my husband, which they don't. You may stay here easily. I just did not know that was what was expected."

Aubrey's eyes widened a little at this speech. So this was the wife that the barkeeper had mentioned; and no wonder he had looked so odd. She was blunt, graceless and strange, and Aubrey, who could talk to anybody, had no idea what to say to her. "Perhaps once your husband returns . . ." he began tentatively.

"He will be angry with me if he finds you have come and gone again," she said, although that prospect did not seem to disturb her much. "Stay until he arrives, at least. After that, you may want to leave again." And she gave him such a brilliant smile, which made her, for a fraction of an instant, so vivid, he again almost missed the sense of her words; and it was not until he had followed her down the dusty corridor to the large and only slightly less dusty kitchen that he realized what she had said.

Here, two other inmates of the house were present. One was a small, colorless, middle-aged woman, with a thin and scandalized face half-hidden by a fall of stiff albino hair. She bustled about the room working her arms energetically, wiping at grimy surfaces and snatching suddenly and sporadically at insects winging by. If she was supposed to be cleaning the place, Aubrey thought, she had made very little headway; she seemed incensed at something, muttering inaudibly under her breath, but what she railed against he could not say.

The other inhabitant was squatting before the unlit fire when they walked in, but rose to his feet with a slow, unbalanced motion. He was quite six and a half feet tall and covered with dark, rough hair on every visible portion of his body except for the flesh immediately around his eyes and nose. His eyes were a dark, dense brown, just now narrowed with concentration, and his huge hands worked themselves into fists and then opened one joint at a time. His mouth, parted to admit his noisy breath, seemed overfull of teeth.

"Oh, sit down again, Orion. He's obviously harmless," said the lady of the house. Her voice was not as sharp as her words. "He has come to study with Glyrenden. You must be nice to him."

The huge man kept his intense gaze on Aubrey's face, but seemed to relax slightly at the woman's words.

"Nice," he repeated, enunciating the word with difficulty. "Must be nice."

Glyrenden's wife gestured to the little woman still scurrying around the room, head bent over her tasks and indignation drawing her mouth tight. "That is Arachne. She cooks and cleans for us. She fights a losing battle with the dust and dirt, though, and as you can see, it makes her very unhappy. I doubt if she will ever speak to you. She seldom speaks to anyone."

Aubrey was beginning to feel he had strayed somehow into a madhouse, but he kept a courteous smile upon his face. "And you are? Somehow I never asked your name."

Again, that curious, brief smile touched her mouth and was gone. "I am called Lilith," she said. "What are we to call you?"

"Aubrey, of course."

"Very well, Aubrey of course, I will ask Arachne to prepare a room for you. It will not be much improved over the rest of the house, though, I warn you. But you will not care about that. You have come to study."

He was not sure if he heard mockery in her voice, and if so, why she should mock him, but he replied at once, "Yes, that is true. A roof and a bed are all I ask for."

"How fortunate."

Arachne did indeed show him to his room, scuttling along before him down a dark and dusty hallway with her head bent to mute the sound of her incessant muttering. The chamber she left him in might not have been cleaned since the day the stones of the house were first piled together. Aubrey actually felt the grit of dirt through the soles of his boots as he walked across the floor to his bed. This was a huge, sagging affair covered with a patched and rotting feather quilt; strips of frayed silk hung from the four fat posters which had once supported a canopy. A delicate border of light showed around one solid wood shutter, but none of Aubrey's energetic pounding could get the lock to yield and the window to open. If the room offered any other amenities, he could not see well enough to discover them.

"A strange and wonderful place this is!" he murmured to himself, as he stood in the middle of the shadowy room. He did not know whether to laugh and stay, or despair and make good his escape. "How much of this did Cyril know, I wonder? What a motley collection of disreputable souls are gathered under this dilapidated roof! Can it be any better when Glyrenden returns? And will I have stayed long enough to find out?"

The next day, however, Aubrey woke to find he could not leave if he would. The previous evening's dinner had almost decided him against staying even one night in this house, so bizarre and uncomfortable was it. The food was not unpleasant, but entirely unrecognizable as any stew he had ever tasted. Arachne served it to them, nearly running around the table in her haste to ladle out all the portions at once, but she did not sit down and join the others. Orion immediately lowered his head over his plate and began to shovel spoonfuls into his mouth without speaking one word, eating huge quantities of the foreign stew before the meal was over. Lilith ate sparingly and very daintily, mostly nibbling on apples and bread and drinking from a large goblet of water. Aubrey ate without examining his plate too closely, and made a few desultory attempts at conversation before surrendering to a silence too immense for even his social skills.

Oddly enough, he slept well in the ancient, moldy bed, and woke up thinking he must have dreamt the whole. He was lying in bed, lazily trying to remember some of the events of the night before, when a chorus of thunder alerted him to the fact that it was storming outside. What little light filtered in past the barrier of the shutter was gray and dismal; and now that he listened for it, he could hear the shriek and whine of monsoon winds whistling about the fortress boundaries.

Trapped, he thought, and got up from bed.

Lilith confirmed his suspicions when he joined her in the kitchen for a light breakfast. "We have storms like this every so often," she said, partaking of nothing but some honey which she mixed in a glass of milk. "It's almost impossible to get the doors open against the pressure of the wind, and it's just as difficult to keep to the road if you manage to get outside. Not to mention that you're soaked through in less than a minute."

"Then I had best stay indoors, hadn't I," Aubrey said pleasantly.

She lifted those incredible emerald eyes to his. "Had you thought about leaving?" she asked. The question sounded innocent but the look in her eyes was wise, as if she were privy to every thought in his head and had been since he walked into her husband's house.

"Not seriously," he answered, giving her a winning smile.

She was dressed in a gray gown identical to the one she had worn the night before, and which in fact might be the same one. Her thick brown hair was wound in the same braid, and her face still wore the incurious, placid look it had worn when she answered the door to him.

Yet he found himself studying her as if he had not seen her before. There was something in the plain lines of her face and the startling beauty of her eyes that was mesmeric, almost spellbinding.

"Tell me," he ventured, "what do you do here for entertainment when Glyrenden is gone and the weather keeps you all in the house?"

"There is very little to entertain me even when Glyrenden is not away from home," she said.

He raised his eyebrows. "Surely you do not sit all day and watch Arachne perpetually clean?"

The briefest hint of laughter crossed the full lines of her mouth. "Even that loses its appeal after a while," she admitted.

"Then what do you do when it storms like this?" he persisted.

"Mostly I stare out the window at the world denied to me."

"Do you play cards? Sew? Write letters? You must do something."

She tilted her head to one side, ever so slightly intrigued. "I cannot," she said.

"Cannot what?"

"I have no one to write to, I have never sewn, and I do not know how to play cards."

His own smile became broader. "Are there cards in the house?"

"I suppose so."

"Well, then! I will teach you. We shall spend the day gaming."

They sent Arachne, furious, on a hunt for a deck of playing cards and any other diversions she could find. She returned with three decks of standard cards and one tarot deck which Aubrey tossed impatiently aside. Additionally, she had found three pairs of dice, two of ivory and one of onyx set with small rubies; these Aubrey kept. The housekeeper had also unearthed a wooden board game but none of its pieces. It consisted of triangles and circles burned into inexplicable patterns on the wood, and Aubrey had no idea what game was played on its surface. This too he laid aside.

"All right, then," he said, shuffling one deck and then laying the cards out in suits. "We begin with fifty-two separate cards—"

Lilith was a quick learner, he discovered, and by the end of the day he had taught her simple games like Drain the Well and more complex games like whist and picquet. She gave her entire concentration over to the intricacies of the game, fingering each card before she drew or discarded, as if the small colored squares could whisper advice or encouragement. She never lost by much and even defeated him once or twice before the day was over.

Arachne ignored them completely, moving around them as if they were not present in the room, and once or twice Aubrey was sure she passed her dust rag over his back and shoulders. Orion, however, came to watch them gloomily before the day was half through, and followed the motions of the spades and clubs, diamonds and hearts, with such palpable longing that Aubrey began to lose his taste for the game.

"We must let him play," he said to Lilith after Orion had silently watched them for more than two hours.

"He is not very bright," she said, which Aubrey thought was unkind with the man sitting so close. "I don't know that he can learn."

"One of the simpler games, then. Drain the Well, don't you think?"

"I don't mind."

So they taught him to neaten up his third of the deck before him and to turn over one card at a time, and they told him when his queen took the trick (which filled him with a ferocious elation) and when his two lost to the four (which made him slump back disconsolately in his chair). Aubrey, who was after all a master of sleight of hand, subtly rearranged the cards so that all the kings and aces magically appeared in Orion's hand, and the big man won the game at last. At first he could not understand it; then he was beside himself with delight and would not let Lilith take the cards back from him when she tried to explain that he had won the game, not the pieces.

"I told you he wouldn't understand," she remarked.

"It doesn't matter," Aubrey replied. "I'm tired of cards anyway."

It was clear that no one else was going to propose another diversion, so Aubrey began to amuse himself with a few of his simpler but more dazzling magic tricks. He brought coins out of Orion's ear (and then let the poor simple beggar keep them); he caused Arachne's apron to lift over her head and temporarily blind her; he took a kitchen knife and pretended to cut off his own hand and reattach it to his knee. Even Arachne paused in her activities to watch this comic performance, and Aubrey thought he saw a real smile come to Lilith's face while she looked on.

They didn't like fire, though. Arachne turned away and returned to her sweeping when he brought blue flame from his fingertips. Orion ducked under the table, yelping, and even Lilith drew back and put her hands to her face in sudden dread. Immediately, Aubrey extinguished the blaze.

"I'm sorry," he said to her a little blankly. "I didn't know you would be afraid of it."

She uncovered her face but her cheeks were still ashen. "I have always feared fire," she said.

"How do you stay warm, then?"

Again, that ghost smile, almost not there. "I am never cold, even in winter. It does not take a fire to keep me warm."

"You are luckier than me. I am always shivering."

"Best not stay here through the winter, then," she said. "For this is a cold house."

That was all that transpired during Aubrey's first full day in the shape-changer's house.

Two

THE NEXT DAY, AUBREY WOKE TO FIND FIERCE SUNLIGHT trying to beam its way past the barrier of the shutter at his window; the air held the rich, hot scent of a truly fine day. Once downstairs, he learned that Orion had already left for a day's hunting and might not be back till after dark.

"Is he a good hunter?" Aubrey asked.

Lilith drank her honeyed milk and watched Aubrey finish breakfast. "Very good. Even in bad winters when there is no game to be found, Orion can find meat. Some of the villagers even come to us when winters are hard, and offer to buy his deer and rabbits. But they must be very hungry before they come here for succor."

It was the second time she had said something like that, and this time Aubrey followed up. "They don't like Glyrenden?"

"They don't like any of us."

"Do you keep away from the village?"

She shrugged. "I have no reason to go there. Orion goes in once a week or so to buy milk and vegetables and things we cannot supply ourselves."

Orion did not seem sharp-witted enough to be able to carry on simple mercenary transactions, and Aubrey said so. "But don't they cheat him?"

17

Lilith smiled. "Cheat one of Glyrenden's servants? They would not be so foolish. If anything, they are more than fair to him. He does not like to go to the village, though, so he does his best to find what we need in the forest."

"If he does not like to go, then why—"

"Glyrenden makes him."

That was all, simply stated, but it gave Aubrey a chill. Lilith did not seem to miss her husband when he was away.

"Have you plans for today?" Aubrey asked her. She shook her head. "Then walk with me. I find I am cranky and sore from yesterday's inactivity."

"More likely from last night's sleep in an uncomfortable bed," she said, rising. "Let me change my shoes."

Five minutes later, they were hiking across one of the forest trails that was only slightly less overgrown than the woods around it. Aubrey in the lead, pushing aside branches and debris and, set a spirited pace, seeking to shake off some odd shadow of discomfort that clung to him; Lilith kept up with him without complaint. They spoke very little for the first hour or so, until Aubrey slowed to admire a pretty, open view before them.

"Very nice," Lilith agreed. She had rested a hand against one of the big oaks that ringed the clearing, and the brisk climb had brought a certain color to her face. She looked much more alive and vibrant to him than she had in the two days he had known her.

"Do you walk much in the forest here?" Aubrey wanted to know. "It does not seem like these paths are often used."

"I prefer the trail toward the king's palace," she said, "but I do not take it much. That is usually the road Glyrenden follows."

And that was another odd thing to say. "What is there to see on the trail to the royal court?" Aubrey asked.

"Nothing much; except, if you walk long enough and far enough, you come to the King's Grove, and that is my favorite place in the whole realm."

He turned to face her. She was not a beautiful woman, but the flat, clear angles of her face continually drew his attention; the depth of her green eyes troubled him. "And what is the King's Grove?"

She had changed her position to lean back against the wide trunk of the tree, and she held her shoulders against the wood in a pose that was almost sensuous. She had half-shut her eyes, and she did not look at Aubrey when she spoke. "The King's Grove is a stand of trees from all over the world, and nothing that grows in this kingdom or any of the three kingdoms farther west is not represented in this preserve. No one may chop down any of the trees in this grove, no one may carve his name in their bodies, no one may even gather firewood from the fallen branches, for this grove is sacred and belongs to the king and will be untouched for so long as there are laws which govern men. It is a beautiful place."

"We must go there sometime," Aubrey said, not entirely sure of what he was saying. "How far is it to walk?"

"Not too far, if you are willing to take a day or two to get there."

"Then we will go sometime."

And she opened her green eyes and looked straight at him, and he felt all his easy charm and all his light nonsense fall away from him. "Perhaps we will," she said, and shut her eyes again.

Aubrey took a step backward and then a step away, feeling unaccountably shaken. Blindly, he turned his at-

tention to the landscape before him, a few picturesque
trees around a smoky gray lake, with ripe summer grass
making a clearing around it. As he watched, two squirrels raced down one tree and across the clearing and up
another tree; orioles made a black and flame-colored
pattern against the sky. The pond rippled with the
promise of fish, and the chirrup and drone of insects
made a pleasant background noise.

"No wonder Orion is so successful hunting," Aubrey
remarked, just to be saying something. "The forest
seems full of game."

Lilith opened her eyes again, and this time they were
ordinary eyes, except for their extraordinary color.
"Here, it is," she said. "You must walk some distance
from our house to find much to kill."

Aubrey considered, and could not remember seeing a
single bird or chipmunk near the house in the time he
had been at Glyrenden's. "That's true, isn't it," he said
slowly. "How odd."

She shrugged. "The animals are afraid of Glyrenden,"
she said. "They do not come close to the house nor anywhere he is. He cannot get near enough to them to hunt.
That is why Orion brings in all our meat."

Aubrey frowned. "I have heard of dogs and horses
who keep back from certain men, but—that is ridiculous.
You cannot have a whole forest full of wild creatures
avoiding one man. That makes no sense."

"Does it not?" Lilith said with a very faint amusement. "Perhaps there is another explanation, then. He is
a wizard. Perhaps he has put up warding spells to keep
them from the place."

"Yes, that is more likely," Aubrey said. And did not
add, *If it is even true*.

He thought she was going to say more, but then a

strange thing happened. The air, which had been still and sun-warmed all morning, suddenly woke up to an alarmed frenzy; a breeze so cool that it seemed to carry dark colors on its back fled through the trees and went skiing across the surface of the lake. Overhead, the heavy summer leaves whispered of all the things they had learned during two short seasons. The squirrels and the orioles and the silver-backed fish had completely disappeared.

Lilith had pushed herself away from the oak, although she still kept one hand on its thick trunk. Her head was turned back in the direction from which they had come, and when she spoke, it was over her shoulder. "Glyrenden has returned," she said.

And the shadow of uneasiness, which Aubrey had thought he'd walked off, hid again under the fall of blond hair at the nape of his neck. "How do you know that?" he asked.

"I know," she said. "Come. We must be going back to the house."

They spoke not at all for the long walk back—longer, it seemed, than the walk out, for Lilith set no very hasty pace and she was in the lead this time. She seemed to have no fear of what her husband would say when he found she had been touring the countryside with an itinerant apprentice wizard. Aubrey's own steps slowed; he was suddenly a little reluctant to meet the greatest shape-changer in the memory of living mages.

But when they arrived back at the house more than an hour later, Glyrenden greeted his wife with tenderness, and Aubrey with a sort of hearty cheer. He was a tall, thin and restless man in whom all the colors seemed to be intensified. He wore a brilliant red tunic over jewel-blue trousers and walked into a room with an actual force. His fine hair was such a sooty black that Aubrey expected it to leave smudges across his cheek and forehead, but his face, instead, was a clean, marble-white. His eyes were a black so pure they reflected points of light from the doors and windows around him, and his long, narrow mouth was as red as a girl's.

He saw them enter the room and strode over to take Lilith in his arms. "My dear," he said, and kissed her with a fine and loving gusto. She stood within the circle of his embrace, unmoved, neither leaning into nor away from his caress, and accepted the three kisses he carefully planted on her mouth. Aubrey, who normally would have averted his eyes from such a scene, could not look away; but the sight of the unequal kisses bothered him.

Glyrenden lifted his head and looked over at Aubrey and laughed, and not until then did he release Lilith. "Forgive me," he said, and charged over to Aubrey with his hand extended. "The servants told me you arrived two days ago. I am sorry I was not here, but I trust they made you comfortable?"

As comfortable as can be expected here, Aubrey thought, and took Glyrenden's hand. It was unexpectedly cold, as though the wizard had just returned from a long winter ride; but no one should have taken a chill in this fine weather. "Very comfortable, sir," he said. "But I hated to impose if you were not expecting me just yet—"

Glyrenden released Aubrey's hand to wave his own dismissively in the air. "Nonsense. I expected you whenever you arrived. But I am gone often, you know. It will be no simple, daily lessons you will be getting from me, for my routine varies by the week."

"I will be happy to adapt myself," Aubrey said, smiling. "I am eager to learn whatever you can teach me."

For an instant, the wizard looked skeptical, as if he doubted that Aubrey would be able to learn much, and then his own smile returned. Aubrey smiled back. He had seen the skeptical look, but even Cyril had greeted him with such an expression, when he first showed up on the old man's doorstep. Aubrey knew his attractive looks and open face fooled people into thinking he had not wit nor strength of purpose. But he did, and Glyrenden had as much to learn about Aubrey as Aubrey did about Glyrenden.

At first, it was not like learning magic at all. Glyrenden piled up a stack of books and bade Aubrey read them, then taught the younger wizard a few small spells and told him to practice them, and Aubrey was heartily bored. The books were dry scientific journals on a range of topics: geography, mineral formations, ornithology, human anatomy, meteorology and chemistry. The magic exercises were simple ones of concentration and illusion, involving will more than talent. Some of them Aubrey knew already, and some he did not, but none of them taxed his considerable abilities, and he began to chafe at the slow unfolding of knowledge.

But Glyrenden, though he sensed his pupil's impatience, was not a man to be hurried. Over the next three weeks he quizzed Aubrey on the facts from the textbooks; when Aubrey was not letter-perfect, he required him to read the volumes again. He ordered Aubrey to perform his spells while he, Glyrenden, attempted to distract him with more colorful antics and spells of his own. When Aubrey's illusions wavered before Glyrenden's assault, Glyrenden refused to teach him anything new. So Aubrey gritted his teeth and buckled down to his studies again, vowing to have the books memorized and the illusions so perfect, not even Glyrenden could see through them.

"To successfully transform yourself," Glyrenden told him one night after Aubrey had managed to resist Glyrenden's efforts to pierce his illusion, "requires a complete knowledge of the thing which you are to become. It requires as well an ability to hold on to the thing you have become, through every imaginable distraction. Say you have transformed yourself into a hare, and you are set upon by a wolf. If you forget you are a hare, and that you can bound with great swiftness to the small burrow which is too narrow for a wolf to enter— or for a man, which is what you really are, to enter—if, as I say, you forget you are a hare, you will be transfixed. You will be unable to move. Or if you move, you will not move like a hare but like a thing that is half something else. And the wolf will be upon you, and the wolf will devour you and you will taste just as good to him as any hare that was not in reality a man."

"If the wolf was after me, why couldn't I just turn myself back into a man?" Aubrey asked reasonably. "Or better yet, to an eagle, and fly away?"

"Of course you could, and you would be wise to do so if you did not think the hare could escape the wolf's attack. But if you do not study the books I have given you, you will not know what it is like to be a man, what muscles and bones and cells go into making a man, let alone an eagle, and unless you learn how to concentrate, you will not be able to cast the spells, anyway. The ability to transform must be instant and almost by rote; and the knowledge of that thing you are to be must be a part of the subconscious level of your brain, or you will never be a great shape-changer. You may perhaps learn how to change shapes slowly and under perfect conditions, but you will not be able to change shapes when your life depends upon it, and there is no other reason for knowing how to change shapes. In my opinion."

So Aubrey read the books again and asked for more books, and learned about rocks and trees and mountains as well as rabbits and deer and wolves. Eventually, he hoped, there would not be a single thing, animate or inanimate, that he could not transform himself into if the need arose. If he ever learned the spells that would teach him how to transform himself.

Glyrenden knew those spells. In Aubrey's mind, there was no doubt at all about that. Behind those black eyes was a knowledge more comprehensive than Aubrey had encountered anywhere outside Cyril's unpretentious house. And Aubrey, whose hunger for knowledge had led him before down paths lesser men would have shied from, making signs against evil, found himself famished for the information Glyrenden possessed. It led him to feel for Glyrenden an admiration bordering on the fanatical or the ecstatic. He watched Glyrenden with a close, obsessive attention; he tried to read the secrets in a face clearly designed to keep secrets; he shivered with delight when Glyrenden praised him, and was swamped with angry despair when Glyrenden was displeased.

And Glyrenden did nothing to discourage this. If anything, he encouraged the younger man's devotion. He used the fluid gestures of his long, thin fingers to hypnotize the young man's eyes; he leaned forward when he spoke, so that his black eyes came between Aubrey and the rest of the world like a glittering curtain; he tantalized with hints of knowledge soon, but not too soon, to be revealed. He had the feast inside him but he kept

Aubrey hungry, and Aubrey watched him steadily, daily, without tiring.

A few times, in the evenings, Glyrenden would take Aubrey into town. They spent hours in the tavern where Aubrey had asked directions on his first day, drinking tankards of ale and talking. The landlord or his daughter served them courteously, but none of the other patrons of the bar joined them or asked to share a pitcher with them. Glyrenden did not seem to notice; Aubrey noticed, but was not surprised. Country folk often feared wizards, and Glyrenden was just the kind of wizard to make a simple man nervous and resentful.

In other circumstances, Aubrey would have set out to charm the wary townsfolk, for he could generally win over anyone when he tried, but when he had Glyrenden's company, he was satisfied. He was even glad that no one interrupted them. He sat across from the shapechanger in the small, dark tavern, drinking in the other man's stories. Often he grew more inebriated on the conversation than on the ale. What he loved best were Glyrenden's tales of how he had used his shape-changing to benefit the king, and of these stories Glyrenden had an inexhaustible supply.

"There was the time the delegation from, let's see, it was Monterris, came to stay at the palace for a week," Glyrenden told him once. "Lord Evan Monterris had come to discuss opening the northern ports to us, but the king did not trust him. Did not trust him at all. But we were to have a week of friendly activities—a hunt, a ball, formal dinners. You know how the king entertains."

Aubrey did not know, but he nodded; he imagined opulence.

"That first day, for the hunt, I changed myself into a falcon and rode on the fist of Evan Monterris. For him I caught three rabbits and a brace of quail. He was very pleased." Glyrenden smiled reminiscently. "But we were surrounded by other petty lords all day, and Lord Evan said nothing to compromise himself.

"For the rest of the visit I took whatever form seemed to suit the occasion. I became a hunting dog, I became one of the great golden fish swimming in the king's ornamental pond. Many times I turned myself into a fat white sleepy cat, and I lay in Lady Monterris' lap while she sat in her bedroom listening to her husband rant. I purred under her stroking hands to calm her, for her husband was a violent man and he alarmed her. She became quite attached to me—she asked the king if she could bring me home with her when the time came to leave."

Aubrey laughed. "I assume he said no?"

Glyrenden echoed his laugh. "He would have agreed, I think, had I not already found out the information he needed to know."

"And that was?"

"Oh, that Monterris was planning an ambush the first time we tried to use the northern ports. It was what we had suspected all along, but we had had no proof until I was able to capitalize upon my useful skills."

"The king must have been very pleased with you."

"He was indeed."

"Other times. What have you done at other times?"

Glyrenden laughed again, back in his throat. "There was the time I turned myself into a young and beautiful woman to charm the secrets from a recalcitrant envoy. He was susceptible to women, you understand, and he told me a great deal more than he intended."

"A woman!" Aubrey was impressed. "But was that not utterly alien to you?"

"More alien than a cat or a falcon?"

"Well—"

"Besides, I had some interest in learning how a woman was formed. I thought the knowledge would be useful to me."

Aubrey shook his head in admiration. "Amazing. To be able to turn a man into a woman. I would not have thought it possible."

Glyrenden smiled and raised a hand, signaling for more ale. "You have a lot to learn, young Aubrey," he said.

A minute or two later, the landlord's pretty young daughter brought over another tray of drinks. She nodded coolly enough to Glyrenden, but gave Aubrey a warm smile when he thanked her.

"It's good ale," she offered. "My pa brews it himself, and *his* pa brewed it before him. He's training my brother now."

"And will you work with your brother when this becomes his place?" Aubrey asked, smiling back at her.

She laughed heartily. "La, no, I don't want to be a working girl," she said. "I've my eye on a good young man, and we'll buy a farm and raise chickens. And babies," she added, with a sidelong grin.

"A young man picked out already, and I've scarcely gotten a chance to know you," Aubrey responded, putting one hand across his heart. She was used to flirtations; she laughed again and wrapped her hands in her apron.

"Sweethearts in every town—you're that type," she said shrewdly. "You don't need to be making eyes at me."

"But there are sweet women in every town," Aubrey protested. "How can I help myself?"

"Questions like that will get young men in trouble every time," she replied. A voice across the room called out for another round; she waved a hand in that direction and bobbed a curtsey at Aubrey. "Back to work for me. Holler if you want more ale." And smiling still, she left them.

Aubrey tasted the ale, which was fine indeed, and looked up to find Glyrenden watching him sardonically.

"My instincts tell me she named you rightly," the wizard said. "Do you indeed boast a girl in every village?"

"Hardly that," Aubrey said, grinning. "I flatter and I smile. It rarely goes beyond that."

"But you like women."

Aubrey laughed. "What man does not?"

Glyrenden nodded at the tavernkeeper's daughter, now talking happily with customers across the room. "That one, now. She found you a fine, handsome fellow. You could have your way with her tonight, if you were so inclined."

"No, I'm sure I couldn't. You heard her—she has a man all picked out, a steady sort who will give her a home and a family. She's not feckless enough to trade all that in for a penniless magician's apprentice."

"Magic makes even the most sensible girl feckless," Glyrenden observed.

"Magic? You mean love potions?" Aubrey sat straighter in his chair, prepared to debate the point. "I've mixed a few in my time, and I've seen their immediate effects, but I confess I find them a poor substitute for real affection."

"Ah, you're a romantic," Glyrenden said, nodding sagely. "You want to believe the protestation of desire."

"Well, of course! Who would enjoy the coerced kiss? Now, I realize a potion is not physical coercion, and the woman who has drunk the drug may feel an induced passion, but I have a sense of justice about the whole thing. *I* would not want to experience desire projected onto me by magic, and neither would I want to believe that no one would love me of her own free will."

Glyrenden shrugged. "Even men without recourse to sorcery practice a little magic in their seductions," he said. "It is, perhaps, merely a matter of degree. If a man has a woman in his arms, and he whispers lies, and she believes them, how is that any more honest than casting a spell? Or say the seduction has been a protracted campaign—a matter of roses sent and invitations issued and, on one special night, the room prepared with musicians and incense and wine—a woman might lose herself in such heady surroundings and give herself when she had no intention of yielding. Is not that a kind of magic? And yet men use it every day."

Aubrey was laughing again. "Yes, but a woman may use the same magic on a man—lies and promises and moonlight and perfume," he said. "And each sex has learned to defend itself against the other's machinations. But against true magic, who has a defense?"

"Only another wizard," Glyrenden said.

"Exactly! That is why the potions are unfair."

Glyrenden raised his mug of beer to his lips. "That," he said deliberately, "is why I am a magician."

But intermissions like this were rare, and came only after very full, very intense days of concentration. Since Glyrenden had returned, Aubrey had seen very little of the others living in the magician's house. He and Glyrenden were often at their exercises before everyone else had even risen for breakfast. Arachne brought them their lunch daily, and very often carried in their supper as well. During the few meals they ate with the others, Glyrenden was gay and expansive, attentive to his wife, and tolerantly affectionate toward Orion. They said little in response, but kept their eyes upon him almost without wavering, Orion in particular regarding the wizard with a heavy, steady stare. Lilith would look at him, then look away, then look at him again, almost as if she could not help herself. Glyrenden watched her delicate, fastidious movements with an expression of smiling infatuation.

Aubrey was impatient with the mealtime breaks, ate rapidly and was always finished before anyone else. These alien soups and stews were not the food for which he was starved, and the strange undercurrents that passed between the other men and women in the room made him slightly uncomfortable. He would have foregone the meals altogether, and told Glyrenden so, but the wizard laughed and insisted they eat. And they ate, and the instructions went on.

Three

AND SO IT WENT FOR THREE WEEKS, BUT AS THE FOURTH week began, Glyrenden prepared to leave again for an unspecified period of time. "I warned you, remember?" Glyrenden said, laughing at Aubrey's blank look. "I said I would be in and out of the house and that you could expect no set schedule from me. But do not worry. I shall hurry back to you as quickly as I can."

They were the words of a fond older lover to his impetuous mistress, but Aubrey brushed them aside. "Let me come with you," he said. "I could watch you work."

"You could not."

"I could. I wouldn't get in the way."

"I don't want you with me when I work." But Glyrenden said it smilingly, so Aubrey was not offended.

"Next time, then? For there will be a next time, won't there?"

"And a next time and a next time. I make no promises, my pet. I have grave doubts. But I will think about it."

The next day he was gone, but when Aubrey woke in the morning, that was not the first thing that crossed his mind. Indeed, it took a very long time before he thought anything at all, waking up in that oversized, lumpy, molding bed. Every muscle in his body ached, as if he had been exercising strenuously; his mind was unfo-

32

cused and unfamiliar to him. The room itself looked disproportionate, asymmetrical. Aubrey sat up and felt dizzy. He dropped his head to his hands to clear his vision, then looked up again, more critically. Yes, this was the room he had been assigned from his first night at this house. Why, then, should it look so odd? It was as if some drug had been administered to his system and had suddenly worn off, leaving him uncertain of the balance between reality and fiction, truth and fabrication. Or perhaps he was coming down with some illness, which had clogged his ears and fogged over his eyes. That was certainly more likely, particularly since he had neglected himself physically over the past three weeks.

He rose slowly, catching first at the bed frame and then at the wall, but before he made it downstairs, his disorientation was wearing off. No one was in the kitchen, but today, unlike recent mornings, he was behind the crowd and not before. Grumbling beneath her breath, Arachne served him a late breakfast, and Aubrey ate as one just lately awakened from a stupor.

He was good for very little that day, and neither Orion nor Lilith bothered to make conversation with him at dinner, but by the next morning he was much improved. He came out of bed with a bounce and joined the others at the breakfast table, and much of his old, easy camaraderie had returned to him.

"I asked you once what you did when your husband was gone," he said to Lilith. "And you said, nothing much. I see why now. His presence certainly changes the place, and his absence leaves one dull and lethargic."

She surveyed him with those unlikely eyes, utterly dispassionate. She still made no attempt to guard her tongue with him. "Do you think so?" she said. "I find just the opposite is true. I am much happier when he is away."

"Ah, that can't be true," he said heartily, pouring himself another cup of tea and sugaring it liberally. "He so obviously adores you."

"Do you think so?" she said again.

"And you must have loved him once," he pursued, waving a slice of toast at her before biting into it. "Or why else marry him?"

The faint mocking smile was back on her pale lips. "Why, indeed?" she said.

He had seen almost nothing of her while Glyrenden was there, but now he found he had thought about her, for he remembered without needing to be reminded the precise slant of her cheekbones and the rich summer-green of her eyes. He thought it was strange that Glyrenden's presence in the house had blinded him so completely to Lilith's existence, but that was exactly what had happened; the wizard had blotted out his wife. There did not seem to be enough room in one man's head to be mesmerized by both of them, and Glyrenden had been by far the closer these past days.

But Glyrenden was gone for more than a week, and during that time, Aubrey felt some of his allegiances changing again. He had always been a fairly straightforward young man, quick to like someone and slow to dislike, and he seldom changed his opinion once it was well and truly made up. But with Glyrenden gone, Aubrey remembered that Lilith seemed to dislike her husband; and now that he had met the wizard, it was important to Aubrey to learn why. Although he could not have said why this was so.

Lilith did not seem to mind that he had ignored her so completely while her husband was home. With her usual mild civility, she accepted his attention again. He played games with her for hours, bringing out the onyx dice and demonstrating how to gamble, carving out a cribbage board and teaching her its rules. When they could not bear Orion's silent observation, they played children's card games with him as well. Then they escaped for long walks in the woods, where sometimes they talked and sometimes they were silent. Aubrey thought about it once or twice, but never suggested they make the long trek to the King's Grove, and Lilith never again mentioned it.

One day they took the downhill path to the village to buy spices and fruit and cheese. Orion had claimed to be ill with a fever, although Aubrey could feel no heat in his head, and they were nearly out of food.

"He just does not want to go to the village," Lilith said, standing beside Aubrey and looking down without much interest at the sick man. She had not lost her habit of speaking in front of the slow-witted giant as if he were not there or was incapable of understanding her. "I'm sure he is perfectly fine."

"Perhaps, but we can scarcely force him to go if he really does not want to," Aubrey said.

"Glyrenden would," she said.

Aubrey ignored that. He laid his hand on Orion's belly, and the big man instantly drew his knees up and emitted an unpleasant grunt. "Well, I'm a passable healer, but he doesn't respond to any of the simple spells," he said at last, straightening. "So either he's pretending, or he's got something worse than my routine magic will cure."

Lilith's eyes sharpened with a certain interest. "You mean, he might die?" she said. She sounded as if the prospect pleased her. Aubrey was surprised; he had not thought she disliked the servants with whom she shared her house.

"I didn't say that. Probably he is just pretending."

"That's what I said from the very beginning."

"But we can't send him to the village in this state. Let us go instead, you and I."

"To the village?" she repeated, as if he had proposed walking to the next kingdom. "Why?"

"For food. And because I am bored. And because I am convinced a change of scenery would do you good."

"A walk to the village would not do me much good."

"Are you afraid to go?"

"Not at all. I will if you want me to."

"Then let us go."

So they walked down, and it was Aubrey's first time back in sunlight since the day he had left to find Glyrenden's house. At first, it was like the morning he had awakened after Glyrenden left: Everything looked strange to him. The farmers in their market best, the peasants in their much-mended smocks, the pretty girls in their colorful dresses, even the dogs and the horses and the well-built houses looked out of place and exotic. He had been too long with odd people in an odd house, he knew that was it; yet it had been barely a month since he had been alone among the folk of this village. They should not have appeared so distorted to him.

He and Lilith strolled through the marketplace like any burgher and his wife, she with a basket over her arm and he with the money Arachne usually counted out to Orion. Lilith was not much of a shopper, for she had no idea what they needed or how much things should cost, but she seemed to get a mild pleasure from hefting the ripe squash and sniffing at the shrunken cantaloupe.

Aubrey picked the bread, and the herbs, and the wine and the salt. Lilith bought a bunch of flowers with the handful of change he gave her, and clipped the small purple blossoms into the braid over her right ear. They gave her a girlish, flirtatious demeanor he had never seen before.

They had just left a small, gaily striped stall where Lilith had considered, then rejected, a large watermelon, when Aubrey looked back to check on some slight disturbance behind them. The small, dirty woman who had watched them buy nothing had thrown the melon violently to the hard earth at her feet, and was in the process of stomping its sweet ruby fruit into pulp against the dirt. She looked up angrily to catch Aubrey's astonished gaze, and glared back at him remorselessly.

"Spoiled!" she called at him, shaking her fist. "Spoiled it, she did!"

Aubrey took a step toward her, almost too shocked to know what he was doing. "My good woman—" he began, but Lilith tugged on his arm and pulled him up short.

"Leave it," she murmured.

"Spoiled it, she did!" the woman was shouting now. "Naught else to do with a good piece of fruit than to throw it away, once such as that has put her hand to it. Rotten clear through, it would be!"

Aubrey shook off Lilith's hand and came closer to the woman, feeling his own anger stir. "How dare you say such a thing about a respectable woman?" he said sternly. "We pay you with proper money for proper goods and you should—"

"Respectable!" she screeched back at him. By this time, they had drawn the attention of most of the other merchants in the immediate vicinity, and not a few of the customers as well. "She's a witch, she is! A changeling! Dogs don't go near her, nor horses, nor cats, nor even the rats of the village. Children run from her, and all good men look away when she walks by. She touches a thing and it's spoiled for decent people—"

"That's enough!" Aubrey thundered so violently that the fruit-seller fell silent in awe. There was such fury in his body, such a torrent of wickedness, that it was all he could do not to speak the incantations that he knew could be used to punish her. "Not another word, do you hear me? Or I swear I will make you sorry you ever stepped foot inside this village, let alone insulted a lady who—"

"*Lady!*" the fruit-seller repeated, regaining her voice. "If such a one as that is a lady, then I'm—"

"Aubrey." It was Lilith's voice, cool and indifferent as dew; she had come to stand by him but did not look at the ranting shrew. "Leave it. Let us go now."

But unfortunately, her interruption had drawn the fruit-seller's attention again. She whipped her two hands before her and crossed the forefingers devoutly; and this ward against the dark forces she held between her heart and Lilith's gaze. "Evil!" she cried. "Evil! Stay back from me, evil one! Or come to you blood and destruction and hate—"

Without waiting for the woman to finish her curse, Aubrey lifted his arms in a blind, unreasoning gesture. But Lilith's hand, urgent on his elbow, stopped him again. He looked down and saw her as through a great distance, rage blurring even her clear-cut face, and thought on some calm, inner plane of his mind, *How odd. I would kill for this woman.* And then sanity was restored, and the world collapsed quickly to its normal proportions.

"Leave it," Lilith was saying again. "We have what we came for. Let us go now."

He kept his eyes on her face and allowed her to turn him so he would not be tempted to look again in the direction of the woman he had very nearly spelled from existence; and he allowed Lilith to pull him by the arm from the marketplace and out of the village and back to the path that led to Glyrenden's house. And never once did he look back, or down at his feet, or forward to the path that lay before them, because all that time his eyes were fixed on her profile, since she kept her face turned from him. And neither of them spoke for that long walk back, and never once did Lilith drop her hand from his arm.

Glyrenden was gone for two more days. During that time Aubrey attended diligently to his studies, back in the room where he and Glyrenden practiced magic, where Lilith and Orion and Arachne never came. He did not want to act as though something extraordinary had happened, so he made appearances at mealtimes and was quite jolly. It was a waste of effort, he knew. Orion gulped his food down and ran from the table; Arachne scuttled around them, bringing in and removing platters, and neither of them cared if he spoke or was silent. Lilith responded with her usual carelessness when he addressed her, and obligingly kept quiet when he did not. He was not even sure if she sensed in him the tension her presence roused. But nothing had happened, really, and Glyrenden would be back in a day or two.

Glyrenden returned in the middle of the seventh night, and Aubrey knew he was back when he opened his eyes in the morning. He could not have said why he was so certain, but he was; the air was heavier or the light passed through a different filter when Glyrenden was nearby. The first few days of the wizard's absence, Aubrey had missed him, and waited impatiently for his return. But now he found himself filled with a curious reluctance to go downstairs and join the mage at breakfast or in the teaching room.

He went downstairs late, but husband and wife were still at the kitchen table. Glyrenden had Lilith's small, slim hand in his and he was playing some complicated lover's game with her fingers. From the doorway, it looked as though he took one finger at a time and pushed it back against the knuckle as far as it would go; but Glyrenden was smiling and Lilith had no expression at all on her face, so probably that was not what he was really doing. As Aubrey walked self-consciously into the room, Glyrenden planted a kiss on the back of Lilith's hand, then dropped it.

"Ah, my apprentice," said the wizard, his lively black eyes examining Aubrey. "You slept late. Have you been holding splendid parties and drinking all night in my absence?"

"No, indeed. I have been most studious so as to impress you upon your return."

"But I am already impressed with your powers; surely I told you that before?"

"There is still room for improvement."

"There is for all of us," Glyrenden said, but Aubrey had the impression he was not entirely pleased. "Except for my beloved Lilith. She comes to us perfect." He nodded his head graciously toward his wife. Aubrey was a little embarrassed.

"You should be a judge," Lilith said coolly. Aubrey looked over at her, but said nothing.

Glyrenden rose to his feet. "Eat quickly, my young disciple. I shall await you in my study."

Aubrey sat down and hastily threw together a plate of the leftovers on the table. To his surprise, Lilith stayed with him after her husband had left the room, sipping her milk and watching him eat.

"You are very eager," she remarked, observing him chew and swallow as rapidly as he was able.

"I don't want to try his patience," Aubrey explained around a mouthful of food. "He can have a temper, sometimes stirred by very small things."

"Can he?" she said, amused. "I hadn't noticed."

"I'm sure you have," Aubrey said quietly.

"Perhaps I just don't care."

"That's moderately obvious."

"What else is obvious about me?"

She had never asked him for an opinion on anything before, and he thought it strange that she would choose to ask that question, at this time, with her husband not twenty yards away. "Almost nothing," Aubrey said with a certain bitterness.

She smiled again. "You have a lot to learn."

Aubrey was standing now, gulping his last sip of coffee and feeling about as mannered as Orion at a meal. "Yes, I think so," he said, and left the room.

The morning's lessons did not go well. Aubrey, wondering why this should be so, laid the blame on his own confusion, his doubts about Lilith, his faint, nagging distrust of Glyrenden. These things had built a gauzy wall of resistance between him and his mentor, impossible to articulate or discuss, but somehow there. He was clumsy with the spells he knew the best, and slow to learn the new ones, and Glyrenden called a halt to the lessons before the afternoon was half over.

"You have not impressed me today, my pet," the older wizard said. "We can hope for better luck in the morning."

And the next morning, things did go better. Aubrey had firmly pushed from his mind all thoughts of Lilith; he had entered the study room determined to do well. He had come in upon Glyrenden creating fantastic colors in a handheld ball of light, and a rush of admiration dizzied him for a minute. Then Glyrenden turned and smiled at him and held out the kaleidoscope of flame. Aubrey took it in his hand and it was as cool as water in his palm, although the gray smoke from the tiny fire drifted into his eyes and stung them.

"Is it not pretty?" Glyrenden said. "And very simple. Come. Can you tell me what it is made of?"

So Aubrey concentrated, and he felt again the liquid icy contours against his palm, and he saw the blue and rust of the burning minerals in the flames, and he knew he held an ounce of the ocean in his hand. So he silently recited the spell that would change an object back to the thing it had once been, and the fire went out and became water and dripped through his fingers to the floor.

"The sea," Aubrey said.

"The sea," Glyrenden said. "Now I am a little impressed."

That was the first thing Aubrey had ever changed from one thing to another, and he was very excited. To change an inanimate object from one state to another, even though the change returned it to its natural form, was not the most difficult part of shape-changing, but it was hard enough, and Aubrey was pleased with himself. He had read the truth behind the altered façade and he had spoken the spell of transformation properly. And Glyrenden was pleased with him.

That whole week he changed many things to many other things and back again. It was easiest, as Glyrenden showed him, to change something to something else that it resembled or would eventually become. For instance, it was a simple matter to turn a lump of coal into a diamond, a caterpillar into a great, multicolored butterfly. The essential truths and structures were in the items themselves, only to be learned and carried out. Much more difficult, Glyrenden said, was to take something and twist it entirely from its purpose.

"But it can be done," he said. "It is difficult and it requires great skill and it can almost never be reversed, but it can be done."

Glyrenden kept in this room a carved wooden box filled with a string of pearls, which, he said, had belonged to a mistress he had loved long ago and now hated the very memory of. "She gave me the box and I gave her the necklace and now I have both," he said, and the smile he gave Aubrey was touched with devilishness. "She must have thought that was unfair, but it is hard for a wizard to lose in the game of love. Or do you know that already? I wonder sometimes what it is you do and do not know."

Glyrenden was talking as usual to try and distract Aubrey from the task at hand, which was to change the wooden box to a crystal one. Aubrey tried to block out the smooth, hypnotic voice, putting all his attention on the jewel case before him, but he could not help but hear some of Glyrenden's words.

"Love, now there is something I think you could tell me about. We are both magicians—we look on these affairs with eyes attuned to alterations. What do you think? Is love the ultimate illusion? Or is it what it seems to be—the greatest transformation of all?"

Without Aubrey's willing it, Lilith's perfect face took shape at the back of his mind. He was so surprised that Glyrenden would frame such a question, his concentration slipped. The box remained wooden and obdurate. Glyrenden smiled with a certain satisfaction.

"Do you know what an attractive boy you are? I feel certain you must, but you don't trade on it often. I sense a certain naiveté beneath your earnestness and a certain shyness behind your easy charm. Let me tell you, there is more than mere shape-changing I could teach you if you had the heart for the initiation."

Aubrey resolutely closed his mind to the sense of Glyrenden's words, though his voice was so well-trained and perfectly pitched that it was impossible to ignore it completely. He focused instead on the silky, polished grain of the cedar box, the veins in the wood that marked its age and its history, fifty years old before the lumberjack had arrived with his axe and saw and laid a charcoal marker across the line he intended to cut. Aubrey felt, as if his fingers were upon them, the oily, creamy texture of the pearls inside, piled on top of each other with a sort of sensuous abandon, the braided silk wire running through their hearts on a perfectly symmetrical plane. As if he had chopped down the tree himself, as if he had been a grain of sand that layered itself lovingly into this cocoon of white, he understood the essence of the wooden box, the string of pearls; and as he understood them, he changed them.

"—But you'll never know, will you?" Glyrenden said. "Because you haven't heard a word I've said."

Aubrey looked up at him and grinned. He realized he

was sweating across his forehead and his chest, but he felt charged with energy. "Look," he said, "I've done it."

Glyrenden picked up the jewel case, now a delicate structure of etched glass, and peered in at the choker of emeralds inside. "So you did," he said. There was a note in his voice Aubrey had never heard there before, and it startled him out of his smiling, so nasty and unpleasant was it. Glyrenden opened the box and pulled out the necklet of emeralds, big and heavy and ripe and cold, and Aubrey knew that this was what had displeased him.

"I'll change them back," he offered quickly. "I had just thought—to show you, you know—that I could do two things at once."

"I know exactly what you were trying to show me," Glyrenden said, and his eyes were still on the necklace. When he lifted his gaze, Aubrey recoiled in sudden alarm, so fierce and furious was that gaze; but even as Aubrey stepped back, the wizard smiled. "Most impressive again," he said, in his customary, mellow voice.

Aubrey was not sure what to make of this. "I'll change them back," he said again, nervously.

"Nonsense, why should you? They are quite lovely—much lovelier than the pearls, and I have no sentimental distaste for them. We shall give them to Lilith. Won't that be nice? Thus we will wipe out forever the memory of that other lover. Much better all around, don't you agree?"

But Aubrey, who had entered the room this morning vowing to trust the wizard completely, was not deceived. Glyrenden was enraged with him for the double transformation; he did not want Aubrey to have mastered that particular trick, or at least not yet. And that seemed strange to Aubrey, who had always found Cyril delighted when he forged ahead in his studies, learning by some fantastic leap of understanding the difficult tasks when he had only been taught the easy ones. Glyrenden perhaps did not want him to learn shape-changing at all. But in that case, why had he agreed to take Aubrey on to begin with?

Over dinner that night, Glyrenden presented Lilith with the necklace of emeralds. "This is something Aubrey made for you," he told his wife, fastening it about her throat with a certain lingering care. "Is it not exquisite?"

She had bent her head forward and held her unbound hair out of his way so he could secure the clasp at the base of her neck. When she spoke, her voice was muffled from her head being held in this odd position. "Why did he make a gift for me?" she asked.

"Because you are very beautiful," Glyrenden said. He leaned forward and kissed the exposed column of her neck just under the hairline. She did not move. He kissed her again, bringing one of his hands forward to cup around her throat, over the jewels, and hold her steady against the pressure of his mouth. His eyes were closed; his fingers tensed against her white flesh and then relaxed, tensed and relaxed, while he continued kissing her. She sat as though he had changed her into marble. Not a single strand of hair fell from the impromptu knot she was holding together with her hand; she did not shiver or draw away or respond. She seemed not to be even breathing.

Aubrey watched though he did not want to watch, and he felt a small stone form in his stomach and make a deadweight. The scene did not last more than three minutes but it seemed to go on for hours, the man drunk on the flavor of the woman's skin, the woman as still as a statue in his grip. Nothing had ever repulsed Aubrey so much in his life and he did not know why this should be so; but while the wizard kissed his wife he could not look away. The knot in his belly was so painful that he knew it would be days before it went away.

Four

GLYRENDEN WAS HOME THREE DAYS AND THEN ABRUPTLY gone. As soon as Aubrey woke in the morning, he knew by his curious sense of lightheartedness that the wizard was no longer in the house. He did not want to analyze his relief; he washed and dressed himself rapidly, all the while resolutely resisting the impulse to think.

He came down to breakfast to find Orion and Arachne involved in a near-silent dispute, while Lilith watched disinterestedly from a chair at the table. Arachne was gesticulating and chattering in her strange, furious way; Orion was shaking his head and grunting out a clear, stubborn negative.

"What's wrong?" Aubrey asked, sliding into the chair opposite Lilith's and helping himself to a plate of food.

"We need supplies and Orion does not want to go to town."

"Haven't we been through this before?"

"Often."

Aubrey ate his meal, watching. Arachne, for all her incoherence, could be very insistent: She held out the empty canisters of rice and flour and stamped her foot on the stone floor in rage. Orion huddled in a far corner and covered his ears with his hands. "No," he grunted. "No. No. No."

When this diversion had gone on as long as he could bear, Aubrey looked over at Lilith with his eyebrows raised. She too shook her head. "I'm not going," she said. "You can."

Aubrey hesitated, shrugged and stood up. "I'd just as soon not starve to death," he said. "Orion! On your feet, man. I'll go with you."

Within a few minutes, the two men were on their way. Aubrey was certain they made an odd pair, he with his frayed cloak and easy stride and blond hair; Orion a good foot taller, hairy as a beast, moving with his disjointed, lumbering stride. Orion was quiet, though, padding through the forest on soundless feet; Aubrey began to see how the big man could be such an efficient hunter. His head swiveled constantly from side to side, reacting to sounds Aubrey scarcely heard—a bird's cry, the rustling of a deer, the rattle of a pine tree. Orion seemed not so much nervous as alert, keening the breeze for every aroma and noise it could bring to him. Aubrey had to admit he was impressed.

When they arrived in town, however, Orion definitely exhibited signs of anxiety. As Aubrey led him through the market stalls, the big man crowded up behind him. Aubrey could feel him jerking away from sudden voices and heard him whimper once for some unfathomable reason. The wizard was torn between irritation and compassion. He wondered how Glyrenden had ever been able to force Orion to come to town on his own.

"And a fifteen-pound bag of flour, and a ten-pound bag of sugar, and one of those big sacks of potatoes—yes, that size," Aubrey said to the young girl waiting on him. "No, I have a carrying sack, thank you very much."

He took his purchases and turned, practically into Orion's arms. "You *must* stand back from me, just an inch or two," Aubrey said, trying to keep the exasperation out of his voice. "Here, load this up, can you? Getting too heavy for you yet?"

Orion hefted the two large burlap bags they had filled already. Aubrey carried a third one over his shoulder. "Heavy," Orion said.

"Too heavy? Can you carry it back?"

"I can carry."

"Good. We still need fruit—ah, yes, there's a stand down at the other end." The crowd had grown thicker between stalls, and Aubrey wanted to get this done and over with. "Look. See this nice place here?" The wizard pushed the servant over to a circular wooden bench built around an oak tree. "You sit here. You stay here. I'll be back in a moment or two. You don't have to talk to anyone, or do anything. Just wait. All right?"

"You hurry," Orion said in his guttural voice.

"I will. I'm just going down there. I'll be right back."

And Aubrey hurried off, slipping through the crowd much more quickly than he could have with Orion at his heels. Unfortunately, there were three women ahead of him at the fruit-seller's stall, so it was twenty minutes or more before he was able to pick out the goods he wanted. "Apples—and oranges—and raisins—and pomegranates," he rattled off, choosing the items his eye fell on first. "Lemons. Wild grapes."

"Will that be all, sir?"

"Yes—plenty, thank you very much."

He had just laid his coins in the farmer's outstretched hand when a furious commotion from behind caused him to spin around. He knew before his eyes even located the disturbance that something had happened to Orion; and he could tell, by the unruly mob forming around the oak tree, that he was right. But the press of people was too thick. He could not see what had happened.

"Demons devour us," he muttered (one of the oaths he had stopped using when Cyril frowned upon profanity) and snatched up his bundles. He was less gentle on this trip through the packed marketplace, using his elbows and hips to bump people out of the way. The shouts from the oak tree grew louder and more ragged, and Aubrey was not the only one moving in that direction. But when a high, childish, terrified shriek stabbed through the air, Aubrey dropped his packages, made his hands into weapons, and tore through the crowd.

What he found under the oak tree for a moment petrified him. Orion stood on the bench, his arms raised and his great palms spread open, ready to slap downward. Three men stood before him, one brandishing a pitchfork, one holding a large curved hunting knife, and the third one swinging a length of barbed chain. On the ground about four yards from the bench, a young boy lay motionless and bloody. Two women bent over him; one was sobbing. The rest of the crowd hung back, away from the wild man's overt menace, but there were plenty of calls for violence and justice.

"Kill him, Joe! Drive it home."

"Did you *see*? He threw that boy down, like to broke his neck."

"No better than an animal! An animal!"

Aubrey shoved himself between the man with the knife and his partner with the chain and leapt up to the bench beside Orion. Instantly, he felt the big man's terror subside a little.

"What's going on here?" Aubrey demanded—as if he couldn't tell, as if he couldn't guess. He made his voice as stern and displeased as possible. "What's going on?"

"That crazy man knocked Kendal in the head—may have killed him!" the man with the pitchfork called back. "You get outta here. None of your mix."

"This man is under my protection," Aubrey said, not yielding his place. "Nobody here touches him."

Twenty or more voices cried out a negative response to that. Aubrey made his own words louder. "I want to know what happened," he said. "Why did he try to hurt the boy? What did the boy do to him?"

"Didn't do nothing! Kendal was just standing there—"

"That crazy man *slammed* him against the ground—"

"Kendal was just standing there—"

Aubrey turned his head slightly so he could speak to Orion. "What happened? Why did you hit that boy?"

"Hit *me*," Orion said emphatically. "With rocks. Hit *me*. Lots of rocks."

Aubrey quickly glanced down. There were a handful of common gray rocks lying around the perimeter of the bench, but then, the whole street was littered with them; hard to prove these had been thrown at anybody.

"That's all?"

"And hit *me*. With a stick."

Indeed, there was a long thin ash branch lying half a foot from the injured boy's head. Aubrey raised his voice again.

"Did anyone see what happened? Orion claims that the boy was teasing him—throwing rocks and such."

"Well, and no wonder if he was!" a male voice shouted back. "That big old half-wit doesn't belong here! Scares everybody, he does! He's mean—and he's strange—"

"That doesn't justify abusing him," Aubrey said, but

no one heard him; others had taken up young Kendal's case.

"That wizard's got no reason bringing such odd creatures here, this crazy man and that woman—"

"Boy's got a right to come to town, see the market—"

"Kendal was just standing there—"

"Kendal never did a thing to this animal—"

Suddenly a new voice made itself heard over the general muttering of mob anger. "Kendal did so throw rocks at this man—I saw him and so did you," said the speaker briskly. Aubrey, quickly locating her with his eyes, recognized her as the tavernkeeper's daughter. "Poked him with a stick, too—here, this one. I saw him do it. No wonder the poor simple man struck him. I'd like to hit Kendal myself most days of the week."

A few of the raised voices denounced her now, but with a little less conviction. She had been kneeling beside Kendal, but now she was on her feet, hands on her hips and a fierce expression on her face. "You all just go on now, do your marketing," she said. "The half-wit isn't going to hurt anybody else."

"Yeah, well, what about Kendal?" someone called out, and the cry was taken up by others. "What about Kendal? How bad is Kendal?"

"Kendal will be just fine as soon as he gets a little peace and quiet," the girl said with asperity. "Go along, now! Get out of my way!"

"Stay here," Aubrey said briefly to Orion, and jumped off the bench. Down among the disgruntled spectators, he began to herd them back toward the market stalls, smiling benignly to show that everything was all right, laying his hand on an arm or a back in a show of fellowship. He was not above using a bit of magic in this situation, a spell of well-being, encouraging the townspeople to cheer up and forget their anger. Within a few minutes, virtually the whole crowd was dispersed.

Aubrey then quickly turned his attention to Kendal, still lying with alarming rigidity on the ground. The woman kneeling beside the boy was probably his mother, Aubrey guessed, and he dropped down beside her.

"How is he doing?" Aubrey asked.

She shook her head. "He's breathing, he is, but I can't tell much else."

Aubrey nodded and touched his hands to the boy's skull, throat and chest. He was not one of those magicians with an inborn talent for medicine, but he knew the basic healing skills; they were among the first that Cyril had taught him. Healing is merely a matter of making whole, Cyril had said; both illness and injury disrupt the perfect and complementary circuits of the body. Find the failed synapse, the broken vessel, the obscured and cloudy patch of fever; remove or repair. Aubrey's fingers, skating over the permeable surface of the skin, detected the surge of blood through the resilient tissues and over the recalcitrant bones. He cleared some slight debris from the sleeping brain, reknit an artery that had split its seams, and made sure there was room enough for air in the lungs. Kendal sighed and stirred, curling up instinctively toward his mother.

"Looks like there's nothing much wrong with him," Aubrey said, coming to his feet. "I'm sure he'll be better by this afternoon."

"Thankee, sir," the woman said. She leaned closer to her son. "Kennie, darling, can ye hear me? Ah, that's my boy, I like to see those big eyes—"

Aubrey turned and stepped back toward Orion—and

found the tavernkeeper's daughter beside him. "He will be all right, won't he?" she asked.

"I think so. He wasn't hurt badly." Aubrey glanced at Orion, who watched him fixedly, then turned to face the young woman. "But I thank you for speaking up when you did. Those men were in a mood to lynch my friend."

She shrugged. "Folks here don't care much for the people the wizard keeps at his house," she said. "They don't care much for the wizard either." She smiled quickly. "But you don't tell a sorcerer you don't like him, or it may be the last thing you ever say."

Aubrey smiled back, liking her more and more. "There's no harm in Glyrenden," he said. "Or his servants. Or his wife. I admit they're strange—or at least, the servants are. But I don't think Orion would have attacked anyone without provocation. He's more afraid of other people than they are of him."

"Well, there's apt to be trouble if you send him to town again," she said. "I wouldn't let him come alone."

Aubrey laughed. "I've been escorting one or the other to town the past few times we've been to market," he said, "and there's been trouble each time. Maybe it's me, and not them."

She flashed her pretty smile at him. "Try coming alone next time and see," she suggested.

"I might," he said.

"And then stop by my pa's place, and I'll give you an ale. And maybe a bit of lunch."

He grinned at her. "Now, didn't you tell me you had some nice young fellow picked out to keep you company?"

She tossed her hair back. "All I was offering was a meal," she said, but she was smiling. "A girl can talk to a man or two before she settles down and marries."

"Agreed then," Aubrey said, smiling back. "Next time I come, if I come alone, I'll stop by for some of your father's home-brewed ale."

She looked as if she would say something more, but just then someone called out to her, waving from across the road. Aubrey thus learned her name, which was Veryl. "I've got to be going along," she said. "Don't forget now." She gave him that rogue's smile again and left him, running daintily through the heavy dust of the road.

Aubrey watched her go, a smile lingering on his mouth. He was startled to feel a touch on his elbow, and swung around quickly to find Orion had climbed down to stand beside him.

"Go now," the big man insisted. "Go now. Home. Now."

Aubrey turned his hands up, empty. "I dropped the fruit," he said. "Let's get another bag; then we'll go."

"Go *now*," Orion repeated. He hesitated, searching for a word; his dark eyes were pleading and doglike. "Please," he said.

Aubrey sighed, but he was not in the mood to be heartless. "All right," he said. "Let's just go home. We'll get more fruit some other day."

This time, as they walked along the forest road, Orion seemed much less interested in his surroundings. He plodded beside Aubrey with his head down and his sacks clutched to his chest, saying almost nothing. Once in a while he looked up, tracking some sound or scent that Aubrey did not catch, but then he sighed and looked down at the road again. Aubrey found himself wondering how many times in the past, forced to go alone to market, Orion had been ridiculed and persecuted. Did Glyrenden know? How would he respond if he did know? Aubrey decided, without examining his motives closely, that he would not be the one to tell him.

But the next time they needed groceries, he would go to town alone. And then quite possibly he might stop at the tavern for lunch; it sounded like a pleasant diversion, and a man, after all, must eat. And it would be no bad thing, he thought, for him to flirt with another woman, one who was pretty and lively and blond. He had grown so accustomed to Lilith and Arachne that he was forgetting what ordinary women were like—he was forgetting, even, that they were the strange ones, yes, even Lilith, with whom he found it so easy to spend the greatest portion of his days. She was strange, and she was married, and it would do him good to go to town alone now and then. Perhaps he would not even wait until the next time supplies were low.

When Glyrenden came home two days later, he was filled with a sly elation. Everyone noticed it, but no one troubled to ask what made him so happy. Not until dinner was over did he volunteer his news, lifting his wineglass high as if to toast someone not present.

"Lilith, my love," he said. "Guess where you will be spending the harvest holidays?"

She looked over at him with perfect indifference. "Here, I suppose."

"Indeed, no. You and I have been invited to be guests at Lord Rochester's home. For the week."

Lilith merely nodded and turned her eyes back to her empty plate. Aubrey admitted to a feeling of surprise and reluctant admiration. Lord Rochester was the richest noble in the county, the king's cousin, and a highly influential man. Glyrenden, who had talked of the nobleman often, had long coveted his favor.

"What do the celebrations entail?" Aubrey asked.

Glyrenden turned his fever-bright eyes on his apprentice. "Ah, the usual. Hunting, feasts, balls, musical competitions."

"I had not realized Lord Rochester was a religious man," Aubrey said, for in the kingdom where he had been born, only the peasants and devout women celebrated the harvest holidays. There, as here, they were observed at the very end of summer, to thank the gods for a good growing season and to ensure a bountiful harvest to come.

Glyrenden laughed. "He is not. Far from it. We are pagans here, or mostly. Faren Rochester certainly is. In the eastern kingdoms, the harvest is not a sacred time, but rather a festive one. I think you will enjoy yourself."

"Am I to go with you, then?"

"But of course! You are my apprentice, are you not? You must learn how to comport yourself at the house of a noble—for, believe me, when I am done with you, you will be sought after by the wealthiest men on the continent."

Smiling, Aubrey replied, "Well, when I was with Cyril, I was in a palace or two. I did not behave so ill then."

"Old Cyril," said Glyrenden with a strange inflection, "would never take you to some of the places you could visit with me."

Aubrey was unsure of what reply to make to that. "Well, he never took me to Lord Rochester's," was all he could think of, but it was good enough; Glyrenden smiled.

"When do we leave?" Lilith asked. She was still looking at her plate.

"A week from today. We had best begin packing soon."

She lifted her eyes. "I have nothing fine enough to wear to the lord's balls and dinners."

"My love, my angel, you could appear in rags and you would put all the other women to shame."

She shrugged and returned her gaze to the table.

"But as it happens," her husband continued, "I have anticipated your distress." In an aside to Aubrey, he added, "Women do so fret over their gowns and their fal-lals." Aubrey thought he had never met a woman who cared less for her appearance than Lilith; but he did not say so.

The wizard went on. "I ordered seven gowns made for you when I was passing through town. They will be delivered in four days. You will be clothed magnificently." And he sat back in his chair with an air of triumph, as if waiting to be congratulated.

Lilith looked over at him expressionlessly. "You ordered seven gowns for me?"

"I did."

"What if I do not like them?"

Glyrenden laughed merrily, as if she had said something amusing beyond reason. "Have I ever given you anything you did not like, my precious?"

She seemed to consider. "One thing," she said at last.

He raised his wineglass again, this time in tribute to her. "And in time you shall come to value even that, my dear. Even that."

Aubrey had no idea what they were talking about, but it seemed an oddly intimate conversation for married people to conduct in the presence of a guest. He stood up hastily and excused himself. Glyrenden, still watching his wife, merely waved a careless hand in his direction; but Lilith looked over at Aubrey with an expression so heavy and so unfathomable that for a moment it stilled him where he stood. Then he muttered something inarticulate and left the room.

Four days later the gowns were delivered while both Glyrenden and Aubrey were out of the house. Aubrey returned first, to find the dressmaker's box sitting in the front hall, still corded with the carter's ropes. He went back to the kitchen to find Lilith sitting at the table, doing nothing.

"Why, don't you know that your gowns are here?" he exclaimed, laughing at her. "Aren't you excited? Aren't you curious? Don't you want to see what your husband ordered for you?"

She looked up at him calmly. "All right," she said. "We'll have to get a knife to cut the ropes."

"Then get a knife!" he said gaily. Arachne, muttering under her breath, pushed him aside when he reached for the cutlery, and dug through the tray herself. The knife she handed him was dull from much usage and no whetting, but it would do, Aubrey supposed, to cut a rope. "My thanks," he said with somewhat ironic courtesy, and waited for Lilith to precede him down the hall.

Lilith's gray dress swept up three inches of dust as she strolled to the front entryway; Aubrey's boots sank into it up to his ankles. "Isn't there a clean room anywhere in the house?" he demanded as they reached the trunk. "You can't look at your new dresses here in the hallway. They'll be filthy before you've even worn them."

"We can take the box to my room," she said. "It's clean enough there."

Aubrey bent to test his strength against the weight of the trunk, cautiously lifting it by two of the crossed ropes. "Is it too heavy?" Lilith asked.

Aubrey grunted and swung it to his shoulder. "Not quite," he said, managing to smile at her. "Lead on."

The bedroom was upstairs, and the uneven surface of the stairway treads gave him a little trouble. The trunk itself was not heavy so much as cumbersome; he banged it against the wall, and then against his throat, more than once in the ascent, so that he was panting a little when they finally gained the upper story.

"This way," she said, and led him down the hallway.

Aubrey had never been in the bedroom Lilith shared with Glyrenden, and once he set the box down, he looked around with frank interest. It was an odd-shaped room, with five walls, and a high ceiling that stooped to a low point over an arched window. There was very little furniture—a bed covered with a burgundy velvet quilt, a washstand, a frayed chair, and a large oak armoire. An open window admitted cool air but very little light, as it was practically covered with a thick interweave of ivy. In fact, the vines had curled over the windowsill and crept into the room itself, snaking along the imperfect seams of the bricks to the place where the wide bed was pushed against the wall. A few tendrils had even dared to twine across the headboard and wrap around the pineapple-shaped ornamentation of the four-poster frame.

"Look at that!" Aubrey said. "I've never seen ivy come inside a house before."

"That's the side of the bed where I sleep," Lilith replied.

Aubrey went closer to investigate. The tight green vines seemed tough and sentient under his hand. "Aren't you afraid of waking up in the middle of the night to find yourself being strangled?" he asked, only half-jesting.

Her sudden smile gleamed and vanished. "Glyrenden is," she said.

"I wonder why he lets the ivy grow into the room, then."

"He doesn't. He cuts it back all the time. But it keeps growing."

"Do you want me to cut it back for you now? I don't think Glyrenden will be home till after nightfall."

She had come to stand beside him and her hand rested, briefly, on one of the flat, heart-shaped leaves. "No," she said. "I like it."

A moment they stood so, side by side; then Aubrey turned away. "So!" he said, his voice sounding a little too hearty. "Let's see what your husband has bought you."

He knelt beside the trunk and cut its cords, then stood aside to let Lilith have the pleasure of seeing what gifts lay inside. She hesitated a moment, then bent, and with a single quick motion lifted the heavy black lid.

Glyrenden had indeed done well by his wife. One after the other, Lilith pulled out the treasures—gowns of green silk, of red taffeta, of black velvet. He had bought her fringed scarves and lace gloves and delicate satin slippers beaded with pearls. And more—enameled combs for her hair, silver bracelets for her wrist, bottles of perfume and boxes of cosmetics. One by one, Lilith laid these items on the burgundy coverlet, and when she was done she stood back and stared at them.

She did not look at all like a woman delighted at her husband's generosity. She looked more like a woman who had been offered two poisoned cups, and had resigned herself to drinking one of them, and now was trying to decide which would be the least terrible.

Aubrey picked up the gown he liked best, the one of emerald silk, cut with a deep V-neckline and narrow three-quarter sleeves. "This is pretty," he said. "Don't you think so?"

"Very nice," she said.

"Of course you haven't tried them on yet," he said. He felt that he was talking just to fill the space, that one of them should be talking; one of them should be pleased. "You don't know if they will fit."

"They will fit," she said.

"How can you be so sure?"

"Because Glyrenden purchased them for me, and he knows how I am made."

It was such an odd answer—and yet so typical of her—that Aubrey could not any longer pretend he sensed nothing wrong.

"Lilith, why don't you want to go to Lord Rochester's festival? I would think you'd be happy to go. You never get away from here, and you should—you should be around other people, enjoying yourself, making friends—"

"I enjoy myself most when I am not around other people," she said coolly.

"I think you're just afraid of people," he said.

She looked at him. "Do you?"

"Yes, you are afraid they will be hostile or sarcastic. Many people are afraid of others, you know. You just have to be nice to them first, and most people are very willing to be friends."

"That has not been my experience," she said dryly.

"But you are not very welcoming, as a rule," he said in a little rush. "I mean, you do not seem interested in what others have to say, or—or to be interested in their lives at all. It puts others off. If people have been unkind to you in the past, perhaps it is because you have not been warm to them to begin with."

"Warm," she repeated. "No, I would not describe myself so."

"And at Lord Rochester's—"

"At Lord Rochester's, there will be a hundred strange people, and I will be the strangest," she interrupted, with a curious passion very unlike her. "I will be gazed at askance. I will be talked of in the hallways. I will be more alone there than I am here. You will see."

"You won't be alone," Aubrey said. "Your husband—"

"My husband will be currying favor with Faren Rochester and his friends."

"Well, I will be there. Glyrenden said so. I will stand by you."

Again she looked at him, that measuring, considering look that he found so disconcerting and so compelling. "Will you?" she said.

"Of course! I will fetch drinks for you and fan you when you're hot and dance with you, if you'll let me. Do you dance?"

"Glyrenden taught me once," she said. "I can't remember why, because he never took me any place where I might dance again."

Aubrey had a momentary sense of blinding insight: Was this her trouble after all? She was resentful that her husband kept her immured at this lonely fortress, away from all other eyes, forgetting the small social skills that made strangers acceptable to each other. It was not that she was displeased with the invitation, the opportunity and the new clothes—as it might appear—but that she was angry these things had not come her way sooner.

"Come," he said, smiling, "tell me which of these new gowns you love the best."

A quick frown swept across her face; she watched him briefly, as if surprised, as if he had somehow misunderstood her and she was disappointed. Then her face cleared to its usual serene mask, and she turned her attention to the items on the bed.

"I don't love any of them," she said.

"Well, which one do you *like* the best?"

She shrugged; now, he thought, she was being deliberately petulant. "They are all the same to me. I like the one I'm wearing just as well."

"The one you're wearing!" he repeated. "Your old gray gown that you wear every day!"

"It's comfortable and I'm used to it."

He shook his head. "I don't understand you," he said, but he smiled, as if he were teasing her. "Any other woman whose husband had brought her such things would be thrilled. Any other woman I know—"

"I am not like other women," she said sharply. "I do not like the things they like or feel the things they feel. And it is better so. I do not want to be like them. I do not want to turn into one of them."

Aubrey stared at her. He was incapable of replying. She gazed back at him and he was shocked at the primitive fury in her eyes. He did not know what he had said to elicit such a bitter response; he could not guess what things must have happened to her to make her say such a thing. He wanted to apologize, but he didn't know what to say. He lifted both his hands in a speechless gesture of remorse, then turned and left her alone in the room.

Five

THREE DAYS LATER, THEY LEFT FOR FAREN ROCHESTER'S home. They were on the road two days and had trouble nearly every mile of the way.

The problem revolved primarily around the horses. Glyrenden chose to ride, as he usually did, but Aubrey and Lilith followed behind in a hired coach. Aubrey could ride, though not well, since his income had rarely been large enough to allow him the luxury of owning and maintaining a horse; and Lilith could not ride at all. So they sat in the coach, along with their bundles and baggage, and watched the countryside slowly unfold.

Glyrenden's mount was a big, muscular stallion, black and nervous, with a volatile combination of power, speed and temper. Whenever there was a strange noise, a fallen branch, an eruption of quail from cover or the sound of an oncoming rider, the stallion reared back in alarm, striking at the air with his ironshod hooves. Glyrenden's merciless hand would bring him down again, and the black would invariably plunge forward, racing ahead as if to outrun some unimaginable equine horror. The stallion's distress was duly communicated to the coach horses, who would strain against their harness and grow entangled or unmanageable. They changed teams three times on the road during the first day of their journey, and each set of hired animals reacted with the same panic and unease when Glyrenden and his wild beast galloped past.

"I can't believe this," Aubrey murmured the third or fourth time they were forced to come to a halt because the horses fouled their lines. "Why does he keep the brute? That horse will kill him if he's not careful."

"Animals don't care for Glyrenden," Lilith replied. "This horse isn't as bad as some others."

Aubrey glanced over at her, but she was looking out the window and did not meet his eyes. They were passing through the westernmost edges of the forest near the wizard's home, and there was nothing to see but the endless line of interchangeable trees. Aubrey thought she was still angry at him for something he had said, or not said, or failed to understand when they examined the gowns of Glyrenden's choosing; but he could not very well ask her what. And yet she seemed relaxed, her palms open on her lap and her head resting against the scuffed upholstery of the seat. He turned his head to watch the identical view out his own window, and slowly the miles passed.

At nightfall, they stopped at a small inn. Glyrenden virtually had to wrestle his big black to a standstill in the courtyard, while three ostlers stood in a tense circle, ready to leap forward and help. The instant the sorcerer was out of the saddle, the horse calmed; one of the young stableboys led it away with no trouble whatsoever.

The hired coachman was less sanguine. He had barely thrown his reins to a groom when he jumped from the box and strode over to confront the wizard. "That'll be as far as I go on this road with you, sirrah," he cried. He was small and feisty, a workingman proud of his skills and his self-reliance. "Never seen such a man for roust-

ing up the cattle! One look at you and they all turn
white-eye edgy! That's it, no further. You'll have to find
another gig to take you on tomorrow."

Glyrenden's face grew cold. "I paid you in advance
for two days' travel there and two days back," he said
icily. "You will take us where I say."

The coachman spit expressively. "That for your
money," he said. "You couldn't give me enough gold to
ride alongside you another day."

"And yet I think I could," Glyrenden murmured, the
tenor of his voice changing. He stared unwinkingly at
the hired man, who glared back in defiance. Eyes fixed
on the coachman, the wizard seemed to settle, to gather
darkness around him; his black eyes were drained of all
light and his pale face lost its faint color. The driver
shifted on his feet but refused to look away. Glyrenden
held the gaze another minute, another. The driver did not
move again. Aubrey and Lilith sat wordlessly in the
coach.

"Another twenty crowns should keep you happy,
don't you think?" Glyrenden said at last, in a pleasant
conversational voice. "Ten now, ten when we complete
our journey."

"Twenty crowns," the man repeated, his own voice
oddly flat. "Should keep me happy."

"Very good," Glyrenden said, and handed over a roll
of gold coins. "We'll expect you to be ready for us in the
morning. Quite early."

"I'll be ready in the morning," was the dutiful reply.
"Early."

Glyrenden nodded and strolled over to open the car-
riage door. "My dear," he said, helping Lilith alight.
"Let us break our journey here for the night. Ah,
Aubrey. And how have you enjoyed the trip so far?"

"As well as might be expected," Aubrey said, answering in some confusion. He had turned to watch the coachman scuffle off in an obvious daze. "Sir, what did you—that man, he changed his mind so suddenly—"

Glyrenden laughed lightly and pulled Lilith's valise from the roof of the coach. "Just my persuasive powers," he said. "Nothing to worry about. You must be hungry. Let's go inside and eat."

Aubrey slept deeply that night, waking bewildered to the unfamiliar sunshine. He could scarcely remember the last time this had awakened him, although surely there had been plenty of sunlit days since he had begun sleeping at Glyrenden's dark and silent fortress. He hurriedly washed and dressed, not wanting to be left behind by an impatient master.

The journey resumed, and passed, much as it had the day before. By nightfall, Aubrey was heartily sick of the interminable forested highway, the ceaseless rocking of the coach, and the stern unapproachability of his companion. The few times he tried to make conversation with her, Lilith was monosyllabic or, at times, silent. Aubrey eventually gave up.

Then they turned from the highway to a country road, and from that to a private drive, and Aubrey forgot Lilith for a moment. The palatial Rochester estate was visible from half a mile away, and it was magnificent.

The main body of the house was four stories high, built of a cool gray marble that, under the moonlight, appeared to be burnished smooth. Turrets rose from the four compass points of the roof; flags flew from each small tower, whipping briskly in the breeze. Every window facing the drive was ablaze with candlelight; the massive front doors, thrown open to admit new arrivals,

spilled yellow lamplight twenty yards down the mani-
cured lawn. Even from this distance, a faint hum of
music and laughter drifted out; shadows and colors
threw patterns against the sheer curtains in almost every
room. The harvest holiday celebrations, it would appear,
were already under way.

"Light, music and gaiety," Aubrey said, forgetting
that Lilith was not speaking to him. "Don't they lift your
heart?"

She actually looked over at him, although her face
was hard to see in the dark. "You are glad to be here,"
she said.

"I am," he admitted. "I've always been a sociable
man. I forget how much I've missed the companionship
of others."

"You have been with us too long," she said. "We are
not much company."

"That's not what I meant," he said swiftly.

"Nonetheless, it is true. Perhaps it is time you left us."

"No," he said, without pausing to think about it. "I
couldn't leave yet."

"You still have so much to learn about Glyrenden?"

"From Glyrenden," he corrected.

"Nothing worth learning," she said.

"You know nothing about it," he retorted, smiling a
little.

"More than you think," she said.

"I am not ready to leave yet," he said again.

She gestured at the Rochester mansion, so close now
they could not see the turrets or the upper stories from
the coach. "Even when you see a place like this and you
remember?"

"Remember what?"

"What other people are like. People who are not—strange, like we are. Ordinary men and women."

He had never heard her talk this way. Until the day they had quarreled over her new gowns, he had not thought she realized how different she was from other women. "You speak as if you want me to leave," he said.

"It might be better if you did," she said.

"Better?" he echoed. He was by now totally bewildered, and any minute the coach would come to a halt and Glyrenden would open their door. "You mean, better for you? For Glyrenden?"

"For you,' she said. "For Glyrenden, it makes no difference."

"And for you?" he asked, greatly daring, because he heard the driver call out a soft "Whoa!" to the horses. "Does it matter to you if I stay or go?"

She watched him for what seemed a long time; he could just make out her face in the glow of the torches being carried from the house. "Why should it matter?" she asked at last.

He was conscious of a sharp stab of disappointment; he thought he made a sound of protest, but it was merely the whine of the unoiled door being wrenched back by Glyrenden's eager hands. "My love! We have arrived! No, forget your things, one of these pretty boys will carry in your bags and parcels. We are just in time for dinner, the man tells me, so come quickly! Out you go!"

Her husband had taken both her wrists in his hands, and Aubrey could see that, in his excitement, Glyrenden had unconsciously gripped her much too tightly. She still had not turned her eyes from Aubrey; she did not seem to be aware that someone else was speaking to her, or even touching her.

"But it does," she said, and allowed Glyrenden to pull her from the coach.

Much of that first evening passed for Aubrey in a blur. They were, in fact, in time for dinner, but barely. Everyone else was seated and through the first two courses when the three of them took their chairs at the far end of one table. While he ate, Aubrey stared avidly around. Between the opulence of the room, the magnificence of the guests, the richness of the food, and the lushness of the music sidling in from a curtained alcove, there was so much to see and hear and taste that he had trouble sorting out details. So he ate and watched, and hoped no one looked at him and thought he behaved like an idiot.

After the meal, the whole crowd of close to a hundred people adjourned to a huge room set up with velvet-covered benches. Here the orchestra that had serenaded them during dinner—or another ensemble brought in especially for this event—played lyrically beautiful music for the next two hours. Aubrey sat back on his seat cushion and listened, entranced. Cyril had taught him some appreciation of the more civilized arts, taking Aubrey to professional concerts whenever the chance arose, so he knew enough about music to judge whether it was played well or poorly. This music was played with all the elemental elation he imagined would be attendant on the birth of a saint, and it enthralled him.

Not until the players took a brief rest did Aubrey remember that he was acquainted with anyone else in the audience, and he turned to look for his companions. Glyrenden was standing in the back of the room, deep in conversation with several serious-looking gentlemen, but Lilith was sitting right beside him.

"You liked that immensely," she said.

He smiled at her somewhat vaguely. "It's that obvious?"

"Yes."

"Didn't you?" he asked impulsively, then wished he hadn't. Lilith never expressed enthusiasm for anything, and he did not want her cool dispassion to destroy the lingering memory of the concert.

But she surprised him. "It was beautiful," she said. "It's odd, but music is something I've always enjoyed."

"Why would that be odd?" he asked, foolishly relieved.

She seemed to consider. "Because I have had no training in it," she said at last.

"Oh, neither have I. But that doesn't mean we can't have an appreciation for it. What do you think of when you hear music like that?"

She considered again. "That music?" she said slowly. "While they played, I saw images in my mind. I saw a careless summer river, white with moonlight, racing through a birch grove and splashing against its banks. I saw the river grow still, and widen to a lake, silver and silent, and in the lake I saw the reflections of every fruit tree ever planted in the kingdom. The trees were heavy with apples and pears and pomegranates, and their leaves were fat and green, but the hour was midnight and none of their colors could be seen. So they made silver shapes against the black sky and black shapes against the silver lake, and when their images shook in the water, you could not tell if the lake rippled or the trees rustled in the wind."

Aubrey felt like one of those trees for a moment; he shivered, and did not know what moved him. "You're a poet," he said.

She gave him her brief smile. "I liked the music," she said.

Before Aubrey could speak again, Glyrenden was upon them. Even in this setting, there was a brilliance to him, an intensity that made it hard to look away from him to other, lesser men. His waxy cheeks were faintly flushed; his eyes were as bright as a fanatic's.

"My love, there are people here I would like you to meet," he said. "Our host, for one. Somehow we slipped into the house this evening without greeting him. Aubrey, you too. You must meet Faren Rochester and his friends."

Glyrenden led them to a group of five men standing in the back of the hall. The wizard, his wife and apprentice were all dressed in their traveling clothes, a fact which became more apparent to Aubrey the closer they drew to their host, for Faren Rochester and his friends wore so much lace and velvet, they would have been at home in the king's court.

"Lord Rochester," Glyrenden said, bowing to a tall, solidly built man of middle years. "Let me introduce you to my wife, Lilith. And my apprentice, Aubrey. We are all honored to be your guests."

Faren Rochester took Lilith's hand and made a shallow bow. His hair was fire-red and his eyes were a metallic blue. He looked to Aubrey like so much ice and calculation thinly covered with a veil of flesh. "Madam," he said. He dropped her hand and turned to give Aubrey the briefest nod. "Sir."

"And Lord Stephanis, Lord Maloran, Sir Calcebray," Glyrenden continued, indicating three of the remaining men. Each of them repeated Lord Rochester's performance, and, to Aubrey, looked much like him.

"Lilith, my dear," Glyrenden said, "this is Sirrit. A sorcerer. He serves Lord Rochester."

The fifth man was decidedly different. Unlike Rochester and the other lords, who were dressed in stiff, well-cut velvets, he was attired in a flowing black robe heavily embroidered with silver. He wore three silver rings on one hand, a silver and onyx ring on the other, and a bracelet of gold around one wrist. His hair was white, threaded still with a hint or two of black, and combed severely back from his high forehead; it fell to his shoulders in soft tangles. He was a good twenty or thirty years older than Faren Rochester, and every bit as intelligent, and Aubrey knew two things before the introduction was made. This was Faren Rochester's house magician, and Glyrenden did not like him.

If the tone of his voice had not been an insult, the wording certainly was. Rochester's cold blue eyes gleamed, as he waited to see how Sirrit would respond to the slight.

The older wizard merely smiled faintly and offered his palm to Lilith. "Here's my hand, if you aren't offended to take it," he said, and Rochester laughed aloud.

"The magicians joust," he said ironically. "I must have been mad to bring more than one under my roof."

"What does a man need with multiple mages?" Glyrenden asked sweetly.

Rochester shrugged. "Why does a sorcerer need multiple masters?" he responded. "You serve my cousin the king, and you would tend to my wants, too."

Glyrenden's smile widened. "I have power and more to satisfy your needs and the king's needs and the needs of many other men," he said.

"And yet, I have always been loath to share my treasures with many other men," Rochester said.

"Myself as well," Glyrenden answered. "Lilith, my dear, you have not shaken good Sirrit's hand."

Indeed, whether by accident or design, Lilith had positioned herself as far from the sorcerer as the small circle of men would permit and turned her body so that she was sideways to him. Now, as Glyrenden nudged her forward, Sirrit smilingly extended his hand again. Slowly, as if reluctantly, Lilith laid her palm against his.

Aubrey had not stopped staring at Sirrit since he heard the name (it was a name Cyril had spoken often, with some reverence), and so he was watching the wizard when Lilith touched him. An indescribable expression crossed that lined face and was banished; for a moment, the man's hand crushed the woman's thin one in a far from social grip. And then Sirrit released her and Lilith stepped back, and suddenly everyone was talking about politics.

But Aubrey noticed two more things: Lilith could not bring herself to look at Sirrit, and Sirrit could not force himself to look away from her. And this was so strange that it did not occur to Aubrey for two more days that, in that strange interlude, Glyrenden had neglected to introduce him individually to the old wizard; although perhaps it had not been entirely by accident.

Six

THE NEXT MORNING, AUBREY JOINED ENTHUSIASTICALLY into the entertainment planned for the day. For the men, this meant a hunt through the fragrant green countryside; for the women, it meant a walking tour through the estate's extensive gardens. The day was fine, Aubrey's borrowed horse was patient, and the hunting was good, though Aubrey declined to take part in the actual kill. Nonetheless, he enjoyed himself. He found himself in the company of half a dozen young men who were nearly his age, and they conversed amusingly and accepted him without a second thought. As he had told Lilith, he was a sociable man, and he had missed such pleasantries in the last couple of months.

They were back from the hunt just in time to change for dinner, which, this evening, was far more formal than the night before. Aubrey wore his best clothes and used the barest hint of magic to make them appear finer than they really were. Then he hurried down to the great dining hall to seek his place at one of the long tables.

He found himself between two women. One was old enough to be his mother, but dressed to the highest standards of fashion; her face was made up and her hair was so elaborately coiffed that he imagined she was afraid to turn her head very quickly for fear of dislodging a curl.

78

Nonetheless, she was charming in a gossipy, knowledgeable way. She pointed out to him a few of the notables at the table and filled him in on their latest scandals and accomplishments.

His other dinner partner was young enough to be shy, and pretty enough to be flattering; whoever had made up the tables had obviously thought he deserved to have attractive company. Her name, she told him, was Mirette. She was blond as firelight and her eyes were a guileless brown. When he smiled at her, she blushed and dropped her eyes, but he saw a small answering smile teasing at the corner of her mouth.

"You can't have been invited here on your own," he said. "Who have you come with? A husband? A brother? Parents?"

The small smile grew. "Oh—not my husband!" she exclaimed, in a breathless voice. "I'm not—I have no husband."

"A family, then?"

She nodded. "Yes, my mother and father and my sisters."

"Sisters!" Aubrey repeated. "There are more of you?"

She laughed softly. "Two more."

"And are they as beautiful as you?"

She laughed again, somewhat more breathlessly. "How can you ask such a thing! I think you would say they are far more beautiful."

"Then I had best cover my eyes when I meet them," Aubrey said solemnly. "Mortal men are not meant to endure such sights."

This time she giggled, and shot him a quick sideways look from under her fair brows. "Many mortal men have looked at all three of us together and not gone blind," she said.

"How can that be? I feel my eyesight failing even as we speak."

It was lighthearted nonsense and she took it as such; she was not quite so unsophisticated as she first appeared, Aubrey decided, but every bit as pretty. Once or twice he caught another young man at the table eyeing him with a certain envy. One of his companions from the hunt actually winked at him when Aubrey glanced his way, then spread both his hands in a brief parody of wingflight. Aubrey knew this masculine signal from days past: "Hunt like the falcon," it meant, and it was always a sign of approbation.

Of course he could not claim Mirette's attention for the whole evening; the man on her other side wanted a chance to flirt with her, and Aubrey too had another companion to entertain. It was late into the meal when it occurred to him to look around for his other friends to see if they were faring so well. Glyrenden was not hard to spot: He sat at the head table, only two or three places removed from his host. It took Aubrey some time to locate Lilith.

But once he saw her, his gaze stayed for a long time; he felt momentarily disoriented, out of place. She was wearing the green silk gown that he had liked so much, and she had taken some trouble with her appearance. Her dark hair, braided into its customary smooth coronet, was pinned in place with gold combs. She wore the emerald collar Aubrey had made for her from a strand of pearls, and the jewels glowed against her white skin with a startling vividness. Her face had been delicately painted—a blush smoothed onto the flat cheeks, a deep shadow applied under the high arch of the brows—and even from a distance, Aubrey thought he caught the faintest patchouli scent of her perfume.

And she sat at the brightly lit table with a hundred people, and she watched her plate as she ate almost nothing; and men sat on either side of her and across the table from her, and no one at all looked in her direction. She seemed utterly alone, abandoned, alien and strange. She seemed to sit in a pool of darkness so deep no one was willing to peer into its depths. Whether that darkness sprang from her or was forced on her, Aubrey could not tell, but everyone else at the table, consciously or not, seemed to be aware of it, and to turn away.

Yet it seemed to him, as he watched her from twenty feet away, that she was more dramatic, more glorious, more alive, and more beautiful than any other human being in the room. The angular face, the heavy hair, the thin wrists, the pale skin, were as familiar to him as his own features, his own body, but they struck him now with an unbearable poignancy. He was pierced to the heart by her troubled incandescence. It seemed impossible to him that no one else in the room noticed her, that no one else stared at her with the same arrested fascination. He could not believe that she was not ringed with men begging for a glance from her eyes or the lightest touch of her fingers. He watched her and he felt vertigo surge through him. If he'd been obliged to at that moment, he could not have risen to his feet and crossed the room. She was the shadowed center in a garish and overbright universe; she drew him in with the power of her darkness, and he could not look away.

"Aubrey," said a soft voice in his ear, and he started so violently, he almost spilled his wine. The voice laughed, and he managed to turn his head and track down the source. The blond girl beside him spoke his name again.

"Aubrey. Aren't you going to speak to me again this evening? What have I done to offend you?"

He heard the words but it took him a moment to sort them out and even longer to respond. This girl he had admired just a moment ago suddenly seemed to him shallow and formless, constructed of meaningless bright pastels and breathy laughter. Against Lilith's darkness, she shone too metallic; against Lilith's stark beauty, she was as insubstantial as water.

Somehow he made it through the meal. If Mirette's continued light laughter was any gauge, his sudden conversion was not noticeable, and indeed he struggled to keep up an appearance of gaiety. He wished he had not been so successful, however, when the woman on his left turned to him as the meal ended.

"Tonight we have dancing," she said. "Faren loves to show off his ballroom. You must excuse my forwardness on the grounds that I am so much older than you, and tell me please if you would be willing to lead me out for the first waltz?"

He had wanted to make his way immediately to Lilith's side, but courtesy forbade him to refuse his dinner partner. "I would be delighted," he said. "You anticipated my own request."

Mirette could hear every word; there was no help for it. "And you, most lovely lady," he said, hoping he disguised the effort it took to speak so lightly. "Would you honor me with the second dance?"

She gave him her pretty sideways smile. "I would. Thank you very much for saving me the trouble of asking."

In a relaxed, disorderly fashion, the guests rose to their feet and strolled to the ballroom, then stood around gossiping as the orchestra members worked together to find a common pitch. Lilith somehow was on the opposite side of the room, alone, her back resting against the painted marble wall. She stood absolutely motionless, her eyes fixed on some point halfway across the ballroom floor. Her hands were behind her back, as if she crushed them between the wall and her body to keep herself from reaching or gesturing. Her face, tilted slightly downward, showed no expression that Aubrey could read. People brushed by her and did not see her; no one spoke to her at all.

Aubrey almost started across the room to her side, but just then the music began. His promised partner took his arm. "Ah, 'The Dance of the Naiads,' " she said, naming the piece for him. "It is one of my favorites. I feel certain you are an excellent dancer."

In fact, he had only average skills, but this woman was so good, his own deficiencies were unnoticeable. Mirette, too, proved to be a flawless dancer, one who had moreover perfected the art of flirting with her partner without missing a step. He hoped he did not disappoint her. He answered most of her sallies wholly at random, and paid compliments so pallid as to be worthless, or so extravagant as to be completely incredible. Nonetheless, when their dance ended, she honored him with a smile and a deep curtsey.

"Perhaps later in the evening—?" she began, and paused delicately.

"I will live for the hour," Aubrey said, bowing. Her hand was still gently clasping his when three young men elbowed each other out of the way to present themselves to Mirette as possible partners, and Aubrey escaped.

Lilith. Where was Lilith?

When he saw her, he endured his second profound

shock of the night. She was dancing with her husband; his arms were twined tightly around her green silk-covered waist, and her hands rested languidly upon his thin shoulders. Her face was turned into his chest, but Glyrenden's expression was plain to read: exultant, possessive, enamored. Aubrey turned away, sick with an unexpected emotion. He had, how odd, forgotten that Lilith had a husband, and that her husband loved her.

Nevertheless, there was no one else in the crowd of one hundred with whom he cared to speak or dance. Like Lilith before him, he found a convenient, empty stretch of wall and leaned his back against it. Misusing private magic in a public space, he spoke a tiny spell of misdirection and turned all eyes away from him, so that he could watch the rest of the dancers undisturbed.

Although it seemed like an hour, Lilith's dance with her husband lasted only a few more minutes, but Glyrenden did not return her to anonymity when the music stopped. Greatly to Aubrey's surprise, they were approached by a tall, dark-haired young man who made a nervous bow to Glyrenden and asked for the favor of a dance with his wife.

Glyrenden seemed amused, though of course Aubrey could not hear what he said. Aubrey vaguely recalled meeting the young man earlier in the day—Royel Stephanis, that was his name. He was the third son of a powerful lord, and considered an embarrassment to the family because he was of a poetic, artistic nature. Royel had not much enjoyed the hunt and had dropped far behind the field as the dogs closed in on their prey. He had straight, fine hair and a flushed, excitable face; he was reed-thin and awkward, but clearly well-bred. And his credentials were good enough for Glyrenden. The wizard carried Lilith's unresisting hand to his lips, then transferred it to Royel's outstretched palm.

It was another waltz, even slower than the last. Royel, despite his other social lapses, knew how to dance. He had taken Lilith in a careful and reverent hold, and he drew her with authority through the intricate steps of the waltz. As before, Lilith kept her head down. Her hands on his shoulders seemed barely to touch him. Royel bent his head over hers and spoke in her ear—judging from his face, words of entreaty and cajoling. For the most part, she did not appear to answer, or even to hear, except for one time, when she responded with a quick, negative shake of her head. Royel was not discouraged; he asked again, and this time she made no reply at all.

Aubrey, watching from his self-imposed shadow, was consumed by gradations of fire. He hated Glyrenden and he hated Royel with a bitter, uncontrollable passion; he felt a profound respect for Royel for perceiving and responding to the fey beauty buried in Lilith; he was aghast at himself, furious and frightened, amazed at the depth of feeling and at the obtuseness that had kept it hidden so long. And he was seared by the sight of Lilith herself, so beautiful, so vulnerable, wrapped in another man's arms.

Royel took two dances, though Lilith murmured a protest the second time, and Glyrenden took the next. Aubrey determined to take the following one. He dispersed the fog he had drawn around himself, and was instantly accosted by the older woman who had sat beside him during dinner.

"Oh, hullo there," she said, smiling with genuine pleasure. "I didn't see you. Where did you come from?"

"I've been right here," he said, attempting to smile back. "Are you enjoying yourself?"

"Well, the dance I enjoyed *most* was the one with you," she said hopefully.

Aubrey forced himself to bow. "Then perhaps we can repeat the pleasant experience now," he said.

Of course she accepted, and they danced again. As soon as it was politely possible, Aubrey relinquished her to another partner and turned his attention to finding Lilith.

There she was; alone again, once more standing against a wall. Had she had an ounce of magic in her, he would have suspected her of drawing a veil of invisibility around herself, for again she was ignored by the people who stood closest to her. Even Royel, across the hall, obviously searching the room with his eyes, seemed unable to find her. But no such spell blinded Aubrey's vision, and he pushed his way through the crowd to her side.

"Lilith," he said, and her eyes came up to his. He had expected to be as flustered as a schoolboy once he finally came face to face with her, but the opposite was true. Sight of those fathomless green eyes steadied him, gave him back a measure of rationality, even gaiety. He found himself smiling down at her, wanting her to smile at him in return.

"You look so lovely," he continued. "I think this is the finest of your new gowns."

"Glyrenden says so, too," she replied.

"And your hair. And your face—you have made up your face, have you not?"

"Glyrenden painted it for me. He set the combs in my hair as well."

"Then he made you beautiful."

She did smile then, but sadly. "I believe that was his intention."

He knew the answer, but he asked anyway. "Are you enjoying yourself?"

"No," she said.

"That young man. Royel Stephanis. He seemed quite taken with you."

"Did he?"

"You know he did. He danced with you endlessly and whispered compliments in your ear."

"How do you know what he said to me?"

"I learned everything I needed to know by the expression on his face."

She did not reply.

"Did you like him?" Aubrey persisted.

"Not particularly."

That was good news. "He seems like a fine young man to me," Aubrey said. "But you should not flirt with him too much if you don't want to break his heart."

"He is a poet, and he is drawn to the unusual," she said. "I cannot help it if I intrigue him."

"I am not a poet, and you intrigue me," Aubrey said, the words slipping out before he could stop them.

She gazed up at him. "But then, you are a little uncommon yourself," she said.

It was the first time she had ever offered him an opinion about himself, and he waited a moment to see if she would say more. She didn't. So he said, "The wizard Sirrit is no poet, either, and you startled him. Why did he stare at you so oddly last night? Do you know?"

She glanced away; it was hard to tell if anger or shame brushed a faint color into her cheeks. "He thinks I am strange," she said. "I told you that most people would."

"And you seemed to be—wary of him," Aubrey continued. "Why? Have you met him before? Heard something to his discredit?"

She returned her eyes to his face. "I am wary of wizards in general," she said somewhat dryly.

He smiled again, coaxingly. "You are not afraid of me, I hope," he said. "Say you do not distrust *me*."

Briefly, a smile touched her lips, pleasing him beyond all reason. "You are different," she said. "I don't know why that should be so."

"Living in the same house with a man makes him familiar, perhaps," Aubrey said casually.

"Does it?" she said, wry again. "And are you familiar with any of us yet? Glyrenden, perhaps? Do you know how his mind is patterned? Arachne, Orion—have you puzzled them out?"

"You?" he continued, softly. "Have I solved that mystery? No. I have to confess I have not."

"It may take more time than you have," she said.

"I don't think so," he said seriously. "I will not leave until I understand."

"And once you do," she said, "you will be gone by nightfall."

He did not know how to answer that, but fortunately he was provided with an easy change of subject when the orchestra began a new number. "I have seen you dance already with two partners," he said. "Will you dance with me now?"

"If you wish," she said.

"Very much."

"Then I will."

He led her to the dance floor and put his arms around her. She was light as an autumn breeze; she felt as weightless as birchbark stripped from the tree. He could feel the smooth fabric of her gown under his hands but there seemed to be no living form beneath the cool silk. He knew her fingertips rested on his shoulders but he could not feel them there. He tightened his arms and the contours of her body became plainer, the brittle bones prisoned in the soft, defenseless flesh. She murmured a wordless protest, and he loosened his hold, but not as much as he should have. He understood now why Glyrenden always laid his hands on her with too much force; for all the power and strength of her personality, there was nothing to her physically. She seemed to be fashioned from the idea of a woman, and not to be a woman at all.

"Is this how you held the lady Mirette?" she asked him.

He was so surprised that he laughed aloud. He had not thought she had collected the names of his dance partners. "The Mirettes of this world live for dalliance," he replied. "It's very possible that I hugged her a little now and then."

"I'm surprised she could draw a breath to flirt with you."

"But she could, very easily," he said. "You, now. You don't seem to breathe at all."

"If you would not hold me so close—"

"But I must," he whispered, and tightened his embrace again. This time she did not remonstrate, and so the dance continued; and Aubrey wished that the waltz would not come to an end at all, but would be played over and over again from the beginning, and that he could hold Lilith in his arms until the whole night fled by.

But it did end. She stepped back from him, and Glyrenden appeared from nowhere. The wizard had no glance to spare for Aubrey. His attention was all for his wife.

"Ah, my dear," he said, taking her hand and drawing it through the crook of his arm. "I have looked for you for hours. Come sit with me awhile and drink a glass of wine and tell me how you are enjoying Faren Rochester's party."

Obediently, she followed him from the dance floor, her fingers entwined with his. Neither of them looked back at Aubrey, who watched them go, feeling the earth tremble beneath the solid floor of the fortress and wondering that no one else in the room appeared dizzy or ill at ease.

Seven

THE NEXT DAY, AND THE NEXT, FOLLOWED MUCH THE
same pattern, though for Aubrey the world was changed.
During the day, the men separated to hunt or ride, while
the women painted and gossiped and beautified themselves; in the evening, there were more general enter-
tainments. Aubrey did not know which time was worse:
the hours away from Lilith, or the hours with her in
company. He did not know if it was more unbearable to
stand and talk to her, teasing her for a smile or some un-
guarded remark; or to watch her, alone and friendless,
surrounded by strangers; or to watch her, turning away
from the persistent attentions of Royel Stephanis; or to
watch her, encircled in her husband's arms. Aubrey was
happy only when he was with her, but he knew the price
of happiness such as that—the harvest gleaned from another man's field—and he was afraid to be with her too
often.

The fourth day of their stay at the Rochester house
passed in much the same way. Like the others, it was a
sumptuous early autumn day, golden and warm; Aubrey
suspected Sirrit of tampering just a bit with the weather.
The evening festivities were to include a procession
through the woods lying on the east edge of the

Rochester estate, all of the guests carrying candles and singing traditional holiday songs.

"A return to the simple peasant rituals, how quaint," Aubrey overheard one man say to another as they stabled their horses after the afternoon ride. "I had not thought Faren would foist off such unsophisticated fare on his guests and call it entertainment."

"Oh, haven't you been here before for one of Faren's festivals?" was the amused reply. "The ceremony is quite effective. You feel like you're walking through the ancient forests of the first creation, having just discovered the magic of fire, and you would swear every tree had eyes and was watching you."

The first man laughed softly. "You've been talking to Sirrit again, haven't you?"

"Why do you say that?"

"Oh, he's one of the primitive cultists—you know, one of those who believes everything is alive. Well, you know, he says a dog has a soul and a rock can feel and a tree is really a dryad. I've heard him go on and on about these things."

"Well, Sirrit. He's a little strange."

The men drifted on and Aubrey heard no more of their conversation, but he was intrigued. Since his arrival here, he had had no conversation with the house magician, though he had meant to, if only to give news of him to Cyril. So now, with time to waste before the next scheduled event, he left the stables and went in search of his mentor's friend.

He found the old wizard in Faren Rochester's library, reading a novel. Sirrit was dressed as before, in flowing black and dull silver, and he seemed wholly engrossed in his occupation.

"I'm disappointed," Aubrey said with a laugh. "You

look so much the picture of the powerful sorcerer that I was sure you would be in your study mixing potions, or at least perusing a spellbook."

Sirrit closed the novel with a smile, and indicated the chair beside him. Aubrey sat. "I have memorized all the spells there are to know, and so now I am free to pursue trivial pleasures," the older man replied. "Your name is Aubrey, is it not? Your master did not trouble to introduce you, but somewhere I overheard your name."

"I have heard your name many places," Aubrey said. "But first from my former teacher, Cyril of Southport."

Sirrit's brows rose; he looked very slightly impressed. "So! You are one of Cyril's students. Then you must either be very good or very bad."

Aubrey laughed again. "Very good I can understand, but very bad?"

"If he sent you away from him because you could not learn."

"No. In fact, I learned a great deal from Cyril. He thought I would benefit from other teachers, however, and sent me to Glyrenden."

"That is just a little surprising," Sirrit said dryly.

"Why?"

"Cyril and Glyrenden were never"—Sirrit shrugged—"allies."

"You do not have to like a man to respect his abilities," Aubrey said calmly. He was certainly learning that for himself.

Sirrit smiled. "Even so. Cyril is usually more discriminating."

"You don't like Glyrenden, either," Aubrey said. "But you must admit he has awesome power."

"That does not make me like him any better," Sirrit said.

Aubrey smiled and spread his hands. Professional ethics prevented him from inquiring too deeply into that remark. "Glyrenden is my master now, and I learn from him," he said. "I cannot malign him to you."

"And I would not wish you to," Sirrit said graciously. "So, tell me, are you enjoying our festival?"

"Very much. I wanted most especially to compliment you on the perfection of the weather."

Sirrit smiled again. "Has it been so obvious?"

"No, it has been magnificent. I understand we are to have a ceremony of some sort tonight, but I am from a kingdom far from here. I do not know all your rituals."

Sirrit settled back in his chair. "Well, this is a ceremony not often observed here, either, but Faren has developed an intense interest in some of the ancient customs of the country folk, and this is one of them. Back in more primitive days, people believed in the universal living soul. They worshipped the earth for its bounty, the sun for its warmth, the corn and the wheat and the growing things. They believed all animals had souls, so when they killed deer or quail or rabbits, they praised the spirit of the animal which had died to keep them alive. Their lives were a constant struggle to strike a balance with the other creatures—entities—who shared their world. Everything was amazingly alive to them—trees, stones, eagles, the stars and the moon. Each had its own identity, its own personality, if you will, and they accorded each entity the respect and courtesy they would accord a fellow human being. More, in fact, when you consider that they feuded with each other on a regular basis," Sirrit concluded with a smile.

Aubrey was fascinated. "And so this ceremony tonight—"

"Oh, well, it's highly corrupted. A thousand years

ago, it would be a celebration to ensure a bountiful harvest—there would be prayers, songs of praise, an offering of the fruits of the fields. Although I have always thought it strange," Sirrit continued, turning philosophical, "that a burnt offering was considered acceptable in any culture. Haven't you? That is to say, if you are honoring the spirit of the wheat for being a living thing, possessing intelligence and a soul, why would you want to burn it? Wouldn't that just be another way of killing it? How would a killing propitiate the wheat gods, assuming there were wheat gods?"

Aubrey laughed. "But the question is invalid, isn't it? I mean, there are no wheat gods. Wheat has no soul. Does it?"

Sirrit spread his hands. They were heavily veined and powerful; a wizard's hands, used to magic. "Wheat—I don't know. Probably not. But animals? Yes, absolutely. Rocks? My guess would be no. The earth itself? Sometimes I think yes, sometimes no. Trees? I am certain of it. The moon? I don't—"

"Trees?" Aubrey interrupted. "Animals, maybe—I might grant you that—but trees? Living spirits? Like men—like thinking, breathing creatures? That does not seem possible to me."

Sirrit looked at him long and consideringly. Aubrey had the distinct impression that he was debating whether or not to say something, which he decided against. "Have you ever walked alone through the forest? Haven't you felt surrounded by a presence much more ancient and much more informed than your own? Have you ever wandered through an acre of redwoods—among trees so large you could not span them, not you with your hands linked with the hands of four other men? Do you know how old some trees are? Do you know what cycles of human life they have watched, and outlived, and forgotten?

"Do you understand how they grow, with their roots drawing up the substance of the earth itself and their limbs stretched almost to the sun? What is a tree made of—water and air and earth and the fire of the sun? Those are the elemental components of the world, my friend. If a tree is not alive, then men are not alive, for we are nothing more than water and air."

For a moment, Aubrey could not speak, and then he took in his breath on a quick laugh. "Almost, you convince me," he said.

"Believe it," Sirrit said, and his eyes were the enigmatic, weighing eyes of a veteran magician. "One day, I promise you, you will know I speak the truth."

Dinner was late that evening, and informal. All of Faren Rochester's guests had dressed in the fashionable version of peasant clothes—leather breeches and vests for the men, simple skirts and blouses for the women. The food suited the attire, plain and hearty; they all drank ale instead of wine, and laughed at the novelty of the meal.

When they were done eating, Faren Rochester led them to the hallway, where servants were lined up waiting. One by one the guests took wax tapers from the hands of footmen, lit them in a small brazier burning near the doorway, and stepped out into the velvety dark. When all hundred were standing on the flagged courtyard, candles cupped in their hands against any vagrant breeze, a woman began singing a simple melody. One by one the others joined in. It was not a song Aubrey recognized, though most of the others seemed to know it. There in the open air, under the huge arching bowl of the black sky, the erratic light of the candles seemed feeble and inconsequential; the hundred voices made a thin, plaintive sound against the overwhelming quiet of the night.

There are not enough of us, Aubrey thought suddenly, drawing his own candle closer to his chest and wondering where Lilith was in this crowd. *There are not enough of us to beat back the darkness and subdue the spirits of the otherworld.* And although he did not believe, as Sirrit did, that the inanimate world around him was alive with individual souls, still he felt suddenly small and watched and at risk.

Continuing with a new song, the crowd slowly uncoiled from the courtyard and formed a processional down one of the flagged pathways that led toward the wooded sections of Rochester's land. Aubrey, one of the last to fall into place, watched the parade unfold ahead of him, the single-file line of torches winding through the twisting pathways of the forest, half obliterated by tree trunks and low-lying branches. The fire flickered; the hands holding the candles seemed disembodied; the singing voices floated back to him, wistful and eerie as the voices of the dead. He followed, caught up in a backlash of primitive superstition—enjoying the feeling, but a little disturbed nonetheless.

After the procession snaked through the woodland for half a mile or more, Aubrey began to be aware of a great light glowing before them, defeating the dark. A bonfire, he guessed, and discovered he was right as he came through the final weave of trees into a wide clearing. The other guests were bunched around the fire, which was huge, as big as one of the bedrooms in the Rochester mansion. They still clutched their candles, although a little less tightly in the welcoming blaze of the firelight, and they were still singing. The heat from the immense fire was suffocating. Aubrey felt it on his face from three yards away, and stepped back.

The movement brought him up against another guest hovering far back in the shadows. He turned with an easy word of apology, to find himself practically stepping on Lilith's toes.

"Oh! You're here," he said foolishly, and just as foolishly smiled. "I didn't see you before."

She nodded and did not reply. He leaned closer, inspecting her face by the fitful fire. It was hard to tell, for she rarely showed much expression, but her face seemed set and strained. The very posture of her shoulders seemed unbearably tense. She carried no candle; she had wrapped her arms around her body and appeared to shiver.

"Lilith," he said, concerned. "Are you cold? Come closer to the fire."

She shook her head violently. "No."

"But you're shaking—are you ill?"

"No."

He could not help himself. He touched her cheeks with his fingertips to find them marble-cold. But he remembered something from his first full day at Glyrenden's house: Lilith did not care much for fire. "Here," he said, slipping off his cloak, which he had worn despite the warm night. When she did not take it from him, he settled it over her shoulders. "Is that better?"

"Thank you," she said.

She had not looked at him all this time; her eyes seemed fixed on the fire, and their expression was hopeless. "Perhaps I should take you back," he said, growing seriously alarmed.

She shook her head again. "Glyrenden wanted me to come."

"Perhaps he didn't know you were ill."

She spoke so softly, her reply was inaudible. Aubrey thought she said, "He knew," but surely he heard her wrong?

She continued to watch the bonfire and tremble. Aubrey moved behind her and put his arms around her, adding the warmth of his body to her insubstantial heat. She neither thanked him nor moved away, and so they stood that way while the singers finished one pretty carol and began another.

Soon there came the noise of booted feet thrashing through the undergrowth, and a party of house servants broke into the clearing. They were carrying a whole tree, one of the tall cedars that were so plentiful in this forest. By its smell and the raw look of its severed trunk, it had been cut only a few hours ago. The partygoers parted with a murmur of approval as the servants came closer; the big tree would burn half the night. Braving the extreme heat, the footmen positioned themselves on either side of the fire, the log hanging between them, and then they carefully lowered it into the waiting flames.

The shriek that rose instantly upon that act seemed to come from the fire itself. It was full of such agony and despair that dread swept the whole crowd; people drew back from the fire, clutching each other's arms and staring fearfully about. A few women cried out. Several of the men laid their hands upon their weapon belts. Lilith sank to the ground in a dead faint. Aubrey fell to his knees beside her.

"What is it? Who screamed?" Faren Rochester's words rose above the general hubbub.

"The tree—" came a woman's hesitant voice, and two or three other voices echoed her.

"Nonsense, the tree didn't scream," Rochester said testily. "It must have been an owl or some other night creature. Are we all safe? Are we all recovered?"

"Someone swooned," a voice said, and a few moments later Aubrey looked up to find Faren Rochester standing over him. He had taken Lilith's head upon his lap and drawn his cloak more tightly about her. He could not tell if she was still unconscious or merely too exhausted to open her eyes.

"What happened? Did she fall?" the lord demanded.

"I think the scream—the noise—frightened her, and she tripped—or something," Aubrey said, improvising, and not too well. "Maybe she hit her head. I'm sure she'll be fine."

"I'll have some of the servants take her back to the house."

"No, I'll take her," Aubrey said, and rose to his feet with Lilith in his arms. Faren Rochester eyed him uncertainly for a moment, then nodded, and turned his attention back to his other guests.

"Everything's fine, she just fainted from the heat," the lord said, seeming, by the force of his personality, to shepherd the whole group back toward the fire. "Lady Calcebray, would you lead us in the next hymn? And Lady Millson, will you help her—?"

Aubrey heard the high, sweet strains of music lift behind him as he hurried down the unlit path back toward the house. Lilith lay in his arms as lightly as a pile of brittle leaves; she had no weight at all. He had no hand free to carry his candle, but he spoke an absentminded spell and called forth a blue witchlight to illuminate the way. Enough of this nonsense, anyway—strange old rituals in the forest, educated men and women parading around in peasant dress. What slumbering gods was Faren Rochester trying to wake? What ancient magic did he hope to invoke? Aubrey increased the strength of the witchlight till the path before and behind him glittered under its sapphire glow. The exercise of his own skill gave him back a measure of security. *This* was the magic he understood; *this* was the way the world was meant to run. In his own powers he had belief. He did not want to meddle with the fey, forgotten spirits of the earth.

Lilith did not stir in his arms until he had carried her into the fortress and up to her room. Glyrenden was nowhere in sight. He had not been at the bonfire, either, and Aubrey took a moment to wonder where he was. Only a moment, though: As he placed Lilith on the white satin coverlet, she murmured once and opened her eyes.

The room was dim, lit only by a branch of candles on the dresser at the far end of the room. Nonetheless, he could see her face clearly enough. What color she normally possessed had returned; her expression was as masklike as ever.

He bent over her still, his hands resting lightly on her shoulders. "Are you better?" he asked. "I brought you back."

Her eyes traveled over the walls and across the ceiling, as if she wanted to ascertain for herself where she was. "Thank you," she said. "Let me sleep now."

"Do you need something? Water—wine—"

"No," she said. "Just let me sleep."

He leaned closer, lifting one hand to brush the hair back from her eyes. "Lilith," he whispered, although there was no one else in the room to hear him, no one in the whole fortress. "Why did you scream?"

But she turned away from him, hiding her face in the pillow. "Let me sleep, Aubrey," she said, her voice muffled and far away. "And do not talk to me again about this night."

Three days later, they left Faren Rochester's house and returned to their own. As before, they were two days on the road, and the horses fought them the entire way; as before, Lilith scarcely spoke for the whole, long weary ride. Everything was the same; only Aubrey had changed. He stared out his window at the rusty frieze of trees and wondered what he would do.

Eight

THE WIZARD'S HOUSE IN THE MIDDLE OF THE FOREST seemed smaller, dustier and more solitary than ever, once they returned. Aubrey and Glyrenden spent the next few days in the teaching room, but the sessions were not productive. Aubrey could not concentrate on his lessons, and Glyrenden laughed at him.

"You miss your new aristocratic friends," he said. "We are too humble and dull for you."

"That's not true," Aubrey said swiftly. "I would far rather be here than at Faren Rochester's."

"So you say now, boy, so you say now." The wizard was making up a small pack of potions, for he was preparing to leave again in the morning, and Aubrey watched him select and mix herbal recipes. As always, Glyrenden was secretive about his task and his destination; Aubrey had learned not to ask. "The day will come when you will find lords and ladies to be the only company you enjoy."

Aubrey smiled faintly. "I don't think so. I don't come from a highborn house."

"But power is drawn to power, and magic feeds on the nobility," Glyrenden replied. The older wizard appeared amused. "You will dally with the king's daughters yet."

103

"Do you really think I will ever be that good?" Aubrey asked.

Glyrenden smiled down at him, a peculiarly nasty smile. "You will be brilliant and powerful, or you will be nothing," the wizard said. "I see no middle ground for you."

Glyrenden was gone the next day, but Aubrey's spirits did not improve. He was so rarely depressed that he was alarmed by his symptoms; he did not know how to recover his lightheartedness. Even alone in Lilith's company, he was not happy, though her presence was all that made the house tolerable. Then again, her presence was precisely what was making him so miserable.

"I think you are very bored these days," Lilith observed to him after he had moped around the house two solid days. "Perhaps you should go hunting with Orion."

"That does not sound especially enjoyable," Aubrey replied. "I'm sure he hunts like a savage."

"Or go into town for a visit. We are low on supplies anyway."

The idea had instant appeal. "We are? It *is* market day, I believe."

"I'll ask Arachne what she needs."

Within a few minutes, he was on the road, pushing a small three-wheeled cart before him. His heart lifted as he drew closer to town. Perhaps that was all that was wrong with him—a lack of company. He had grown accustomed to agreeable society during his stay at Faren Rochester's, and he missed it now. He was unused to being alone—or nearly alone, with only two strange servants to chaperone him while he kept company with the shape-changer's wife. Any man would feel restless and on edge under such circumstances. What he needed was interaction with ordinary men and women, just the sort of people he was likely to find in the village.

As always on market day, the square was crowded with farmers come to sell their produce and townspeople shopping for household goods. Aubrey maneuvered his cart carefully through the throng, apologizing frequently for grazing someone's ankle or hip. He took his time about making purchases, engaging each entrepreneur in a lengthy debate about the merits of red apples over green, white rice over brown, yellow potatoes over white.

"Well, for your pies—your pies, now, they're best made with green apples," a fat-cheeked old woman told him. "They're a little sour for eating, but you sugar them up right, bake them in a crust, and they're just as sweet as molasses. Can you make a pie, sir?"

"I?" Aubrey laughed. "Well, I never have made one. I'm not a stupid man, though. I suppose I could make one if I tried."

She smiled at him out of the smallest, bluest eyes he'd ever seen. "Oh, you've got a woman as cooks for you," she said, nodding wisely. "Well, that's the best way, ain't it? Having somebody to care for you."

"Having somebody to care for," he returned lightly.

She leaned closer and motioned him to bend down. Aubrey brought his ear to her mouth. "Down there a ways—see it? The stall with the black awning. Man there is selling things you might want to look at."

"What things?" Aubrey said.

"Ssh! Not everyone is to know. Pieces of gold, you know, rings and bracelets that a man might give to a lady. You've got a lady to give them to?"

Aubrey thought of Lilith, reflexively; then, with deter-

mination, of the tavernkeeper's blond daughter. "Yes,"
he said.

"Then go take a look. They've got mighty pretty
things there." And she drew back and smiled at him; and
he straightened up and smiled back.

Of course, with her eyes on him, he had to wend his
way directly to the jeweler's stall. He had no real intention of buying anything, but it couldn't hurt to look. He
owed the old woman that much for telling him the secret.

On first inspection, however, the jeweler's goods did
not impress him. There were a few cheap pewter rings
set with cut glass; wax beads had been painted with an
oily substance to give them the lustre of pearls. For
courtesy's sake, Aubrey poked at a necklace or two, but
he shook his head when the dark young man behind the
counter asked if there was anything he particularly liked.

"I was told—the fruit-seller from down the way—she
said you had some gold jewelry I might like," Aubrey
said. "But I'm afraid I don't see anything here—"

"Ah, the gold pieces," the young man said quickly.
He had an odd, indefinable accent; even Aubrey, who
had traveled some, could not place it. "We keep them in
back. Not everyone we meet can afford them." The
young man disappeared behind a heavy curtain, reap-
pearing in a few moments with a black velvet tray in one
hand. "Were you more interested in something like
this?" he asked.

Aubrey's silent admiration was answer enough. He
had learned enough about gold, in his studies of shape-
changing, to appreciate the quality of these items. The
thick chains lay almost languorously on the black velvet,
twisted here and there in voluptuous disarray. Aubrey
picked gently through the bracelets and braided rings

and ankle chains, and finally rested his fingers on a short gold necklace. It was wide and flat and sinuous; it would lie like a band of light across a woman's throat. The clasp was studded with three diamonds set in a triangular pattern.

"I think this may be the one I cannot live without," Aubrey said, holding it up till it caught the sunlight. "I warn you, though, that I am a wizard of great skill. If its price is too high, I shall have to turn you into a monkey, and then you shall look very silly trying to sell your gold."

The young man grinned, unalarmed, but he did look interested. "Is that right? A wizard? Well, now—but perhaps you aren't willing to trade your talent for gold."

Aubrey smiled and laid the necklace reluctantly aside. "I've traded it for less," he said cheerfully. "What do you need done?"

The jeweler looked, all at once, much younger and much less self-assured. "It's my father. He usually comes with me when we journey to the markets, but he's been ill—oh, a month or two. I hated to leave him, but sales in the city are so slow these days. Well, you know how it is, silver's become the only thing the fashionable women will wear, and of course we haven't any connections at the silver mines. So we come on the road, and we sell the gaudy pieces to the peasant folk and the gold to the lords and ladies. And I had to leave, but I hated to go, with him being so sick—"

"Is it a potion you need?" Aubrey interrupted. "I can mix you one, if you know what his sickness is."

"Lung sickness," the young man said. "He gets it every year. But—could you do something more? I've heard that wizards can look into a cup of water and call up visions. Could you do that? Could you tell me how he is, right now, today?"

"Well, not in a cup of water," Aubrey said. He glanced quickly around the array of costume jewelry spread out at the front of the booth. He remembered an ugly pewter ring set with a huge glass marble; hardly an ideal scrying crystal, but for something this simple, it would do. Aubrey picked up the ring and slipped it over the smallest finger on his left hand.

"Here," he said. "Let's see what we can discover."

Scrying was the first thing Aubrey had learned. Cyril was, by far, the best magician in the three kingdoms at this particular skill, and Aubrey had found it an easy enough ritual to master. Now he questioned the young man ("Where are you from? What is your father's name? Describe your house to me") while he passed his hand over the smooth surface of the glass. Soon enough, wavering colors formed in the heart of the globe and resolved themselves into shapes. Aubrey studied the tiny, moving forms, then held his hand out to the jeweler.

"See for yourself," he invited.

The young man, who had identified himself as Benni Rosta, looked dubious a moment, and then leaned forward to peer into the glass. He drew a sharp, quick breath. "That's my father!" he exclaimed. "And he's—he's sitting up; he's talking to someone. That must be—oh yes, that's my aunt there with him. She must be caring for him while I'm gone." Benni looked radiantly over at Aubrey. "He's better," he said.

Aubrey took off the ring. Instantly, the shadowy shapes melted and disappeared. "It looks that way," he said. "You say he has this lung trouble often?"

Benni nodded. "Every year it gets worse," he said.

"The town doctors have given him drugs, but nothing seems to help. This year—this is as bad as I've seen it."

Aubrey nodded. "Do you have a flask of water you can spare?" he asked. "Something you won't need on your journey?"

"I suppose I do. Surely." Benni looked inquiring.

"I can lay an enchantment upon the water," Aubrey explained. "Then your father can drink it, a little at a time when he grows ill, and it will heal his lungs. It should last him a long time—he shouldn't have to drink more than a cupful once a year to turn the sickness away."

Benni was regarding him with astonished, disbelieving eyes. "You can do that?" he breathed.

Aubrey smiled. "Yes," he said, "if you have the flask of water."

What Benni gave him was a two-gallon jug made of heavy clay and corked tight. "Very good," Aubrey said, and unsealed it. He inserted his finger into the mouth of the jug, just dipping it into the water, and silently recited the proper spell. This one, too, he had learned early; Cyril's favorite patron had been a kindly old woman who suffered from troubled breathing, and Cyril had been at pains to keep her healthy.

Benni, however, looked slightly skeptical. "And this will really heal him?" he asked. "This—a drink of this water—"

"It is not an herbal remedy such as the doctors make," Aubrey admitted. "It will look like water, and it will taste like water. But it will ease him. I cannot prove it to you now, but you may believe me."

"I saw his face in my glass ring," Benni said. "I believe you."

When they were finished with magic, they turned to

finance, haggling over the cost of the jewelry. Benni declared that Aubrey's services were worth the entire price of the necklace, if not more; Aubrey insisted on paying him a few coins, nonetheless, because he didn't feel he had worked hard enough to earn such a fee. In the end, they parted happy, each of them convinced he had gotten the better part of the deal, and Aubrey additionally buoyed by the gratification of having done a service to another human being.

In this beneficent mood, he trundled his cart over to the tavern, parked it outside, spoke a few anti-theft words over it, and entered the warm, dark room. He took a seat in a booth near the back, nodding at the other patrons as he passed their tables. In a very few minutes, Veryl approached him, carrying a tankard of ale.

"So! The wizard's household needed supplies," she said. "I wondered if you might be stopping by one day."

"It seemed better if I came alone," Aubrey said, smiling up at her. "You were right."

"So it's lunch you want this time?"

"You told me you'd feed me. Don't you remember?"

She laughed at him. "I remember. Will you have ham or beef?"

Both sounded suddenly good. At Glyrenden's, they ate mostly game—venison and rabbit and quail, the meat that Orion brought in. "Ham, I think," said Aubrey. "And anything that might go with it."

She was back in five minutes, carrying two plates. When she set the second one down, she slid into the booth across from him.

"My lunch time too," she said. "It's hungry work."

They ate in companionable silence for a few moments, but Aubrey was marveling inwardly at how much she consumed. Lilith took in virtually no sustenance from morning till night, and he had yet to see Arachne eat anything. He had forgotten that women had appetites as hearty as a man's.

"So what did you buy today?" she asked, when she was through with the greatest portion of her food.

He thought of the short gold chain, curled sleepily in its red velvet bag. "Oh, the usual items," he said. "Rice and sugar and potatoes."

She shook her head. "Prices are terrible," she said. "Farmers lost crops in the drought, I know it, but they think they can charge the townspeople absolutely anything they want. We grow our own crops a few miles outside of town, and lucky for us! I don't think we could afford to keep our doors open if we had to buy at market prices."

"I know very little about pricing vegetables," Aubrey said.

"Oh, we used to run a stall in the market, back before my pa had the tavern," Veryl said. "Mostly fruit and corn, but then we started growing wheat when Pa bought up old man Russet's farm. I didn't work in the fields— Pa hired boys to do that—but I sure worked at the market, I can tell you. Bright and early! Setting up the awning, laying out the fruit. Don't let anybody tell you it isn't hard work."

Aubrey would not have believed that she could talk so much. That anyone could talk so much. All he had to do was murmur an assent now and then, or give a brief answer to a sudden, swift question, and she was off again, chattering away. He kept an expression of interest on his face, but he was wondering how long he would have to sit there listening to her. The exaggerated expressiveness of her face annoyed him, too—she laughed, grimaced, scowled and raised her eyebrows with nearly every sen-

tence, as if she were enacting a pantomime to under-
score the sense of her words. Aubrey felt his face muscles grow weary as he kept his smile in place.

"Not easy running around waiting on all the men of
the village, either," she was saying. "But at least it's indoors, so rain or shine doesn't matter a bit! At the market, we were there winter and summer, wet weather or
cold. And let me tell you, there were some cold, wet
days I stood in the stall selling apples."

"Veryl!" The call came from the other side of the
room—a man's voice, surely her father's. Veryl jumped
up and scooped her plate and glass into her hands.

"Looks like lunch is over," she said, grinning down at
Aubrey. "But it was a fun one, wasn't it?"

"Very pleasant," Aubrey acknowledged. "I'm glad
you could join me."

"Oh, I get an hour off now and then," she said airily.

"Veryl!" Her father's voice sounded more impatient.

"Next time," she said, and skipped back toward the
kitchen, laughing as she went.

Aubrey quickly drained the last drops of ale from his
tankard, laid his money on the table and extricated himself from the booth. As fast as he could manage it without appearing to run, he was back outside and once more
on the forest road. He did not want to think about it, so
he closed his mind to the implications of the afternoon,
but he knew at least one thing for certain: He might return to town again and again; he might come for supplies or drop in for companionship; he might even spend
another thirty minutes listening to the tavernkeeper's
daughter telling him the story of her life. But there was
nothing here that held any lasting appeal for him, nothing here he cared much about—nothing that could lure
him from Glyrenden's cold gray fortress for more than

an afternoon or make him forget its inhabitants even for an hour.

That night at dinner, Aubrey gave the necklace to Lilith. Orion had already finished his portion and lumbered back to his corner to sleep. Arachne was cleaning around them, clucking and hissing at the mess they had made. Once, as Lilith reached out for her glass, Arachne's hand slammed down on the table beside it, causing Lilith to pause just a moment before she picked up her honeyed milk.

"A fly," Lilith said in unconcern as Aubrey looked over, surprised. "Arachne hates them."

Aubrey had thought of any number of ways to make this presentation to Lilith, but in the end, they all seemed foolish. *I bought you this lovely gift because you yourself are so lovely . . . I think of you, I dream of you, I want you to remember me—take this gift from my hands. . . .* He reached into his pocket and pulled out the red velvet bag.

"Here," he said, handing it to her across the table. "I bought you something in town."

Incurious, she took it from him and spilled the contents into her palm. The gold chain uncoiled and preened in her hand. "A necklace," she said. "Why, thank you, Aubrey."

"I did a service for a jeweler at the market," Aubrey said. "He gave me the necklace in return."

"Shall I wear it now?"

"Oh yes."

She clasped it around her neck, having a moment of difficulty with the diamond-studded clasp. It lay glittering and incongruous across the dull gray cotton of her high-necked gown. "How does that look?" she asked.

"Very fine," Aubrey said. It did not; it looked ridiculous and out of place. Yet still Aubrey felt an illicit pleasure in giving this woman a beautiful gift. "I hope you wear it as often as you like."

She fingered the fine satin length of gold. "Glyrenden might wonder where I got it," she said.

Aubrey laughed. "I'll tell him I was practicing my shape-changer's skills and that I made it for you from a length of string."

"Will he believe you?"

"You mean, is that something I am capable of doing?"

"I suppose."

"Certainly I can. He taught me how himself."

"Then there is no reason he should not believe you."

They did not talk about the necklace again that night, or ever, but Aubrey was pleased to see that Lilith wore it every day for a week. One morning, she appeared at the breakfast table without it, and that afternoon Glyrenden returned home. She did not wear it again for two more days, by which time her husband was gone once again.

Nine

AUBREY COULD NOT TELL IF HE WAS GLAD OR SORRY when Glyrenden told them that he had only come home for a brief two-day visit. The distrust Glyrenden had inspired in him so early had become a settled and accepted thing, at least in his own mind, and yet he still had great admiration for the older wizard's powers—and an unquenchable desire to learn everything Glyrenden might be willing to teach him. Not only that, he was in love with the shape-changer's wife, which made it difficult for him when Glyrenden appeared at the breakfast table in the guise of a husband. Yet Aubrey, clinging still to rational thought, realized it was no bad thing for him to be reminded now and then that the woman had a husband—for she did have a husband—and when Glyrenden was gone, Aubrey was in danger of forgetting that fact.

So he was able to summon up real dismay when Glyrenden said he would be returning very shortly to the king's palace.

"So soon?" Aubrey questioned. "You are rarely here these days."

"And will be gone again and yet again in the next month or two, for events move rapidly at court," the mage replied. He was sorting through bags of crystals

115

and looking up formulas in spellbooks; he seemed abstracted but not irritated by Aubrey's company.

"More shape-changing?" Aubrey asked.

Glyrenden looked over with a smile of excitement. "Not this trip," he said. "This is one of those times when illusion stands me in better stead than alteration."

"We have not practiced illusions since I first arrived," Aubrey said.

Glyrenden laughed. "Have we not? Then you must let me show you a trick or two."

The wizard strode to the doorway. "Orion! Arachne! Come here a moment. I have need of you."

Aubrey's eyes widened, for generally Glyrenden invited no one into his study except his apprentice. He misliked the wizard's mood, so maliciously elated, and wondered what was really going on up at the royal court. Not for the first time, he found himself feeling a certain disapproval of the king and his methods.

Orion and Arachne entered, the man behind the woman, neither of them looking pleased to be called. Arachne cast furtive glances around the room, gauging its disorder and dust content; Orion dragged his feet reluctantly across the flagged floor and kept his eyes on Glyrenden's face.

"Don't be so apprehensive, nothing is going to happen to you," Glyrenden told the big man in a chiding voice. "Just stand there, both of you—just like that. Fine. Try not to move if you can help it. An unattractive pair, aren't they?" the sorcerer continued, scarcely dropping his voice as he turned to address Aubrey. "Does it turn your stomach to take meat from her hands or share the table with him?"

Aubrey was so appalled at the casual cruelty, he scarcely knew how to answer. "No! I mean—they look fine to me," he said lamely. "Not every man or woman is beautiful."

"But magic could make them so," Glyrenden said. "*I* could have made them so. I can make them beautiful now. Watch."

The wizard had lifted his hands as he spoke; now, with a single liquid motion, he flicked his fingers in the air and dropped his hands. Both fascinated and repulsed, Aubrey kept his attention on the two servants. For a moment, their faces seemed to waver, or to take on a faint, luminescent glow; and then the haze evaporated and he could see them clearly again. Or perhaps not . . .

Orion's massive, hairy face had been remodeled, slimmed down; he still had wide cheeks and a large forehead, but he looked like any other brawny, full-bearded man of moderate intelligence. Arachne's small, angry countenance had smoothed out and warmed up. Her white hair had been pulled back and given an attractive golden sheen. Like Orion, she resembled any other peasant one might pass on the road—not lovely, certainly, but hardly extraordinary. Not at all strange.

"What have you done?" Aubrey asked, as much in fear as wonder.

"Oh, merely a little sleight of hand," was the negligent reply. "A deception, not a transformation. You see?" Glyrenden spread his fingers again, and the illusion vanished. Back in their familiar shapes were the two homely creatures, still waiting patiently to do whatever their master bid them. Glyrenden smiled. "A momentary aberration only. You may go now," he said, addressing his servants, and the man and woman left the room.

"Most impressive," Aubrey said, because he must say

something. "You are as good at that as you are at everything."

Glyrenden laughed again, almost indulgently, it seemed. "Oh, I prefer out-and-out alchemy," he said, "but there are many instances in which it is not appropriate. Then again, you would be surprised at how many people believe an illusion, even when the illusion is ripped away. They are as likely to believe that the false face is the true one and that the true one is the one that has been bewitched."

"How is one ever to know the difference, then?" Aubrey asked, keeping his voice even.

Glyrenden spread his hands as if to signify that he did not know. "And does it matter?" he asked softly. "When disguise is preferable to the hard bare bones of reality?"

"It matters," Aubrey said.

"You had best be prepared for some unpleasant surprises if you constantly seek the kernel of truth," Glyrenden advised.

"But magic is founded on truth," Aubrey said. "Without an understanding of what a thing really is, it cannot be either uncovered or changed."

"But the heart of magic is illusion," Glyrenden said. "And without the cooperation of gullible men, there would be no magic at all."

Glyrenden was gone by nightfall, but his disturbing words lingered, as did the memory of the masks he had created for the faces of his servants. At the breakfast table the next day, Aubrey found himself still brooding over Glyrenden's demonstration, and watching both Orion and Arachne with closer attention than he had given them for weeks. He was not sure why he was suddenly so intent, what he expected to read in their stubborn, familiar faces. They had not, after all, been permanently altered in Glyrenden's study. They were the same as they had always been—and yet—and yet—

Arachne came around the table one more time with her curious, sideways motion, her arms working so rapidly it almost seemed she had four arms, eight arms; certainly more than her allotted two. Her bleached skin was of the oddest texture, tougher than skin should be, with a faint sheen upon it that was not perspiration. Aubrey looked up at her face, trying to get a glimpse of her eyes, but she was turned away from him, and would not look in his direction. She whispered baleful words at him as she whisked past, the strange garbled sentences making no sense, as they never made any sense.

Orion, as usual, had finished his meal with an indecent haste, then rose to his feet with a slow, unbalanced motion as if the act dizzied him. He shook his head so violently, his whole body trembled; then he gave a great yawn that exposed his large, sharp teeth. No one spoke to him; Aubrey's troubled gaze aroused his anger and he stared back menacingly enough to cause the young man to look away. Orion waited a moment, as if expecting orders. When none came, he shook himself again, then lumbered over to his cot and stretched himself out on it full length. Within minutes, he was asleep.

Together they were a strange woman and a strange man, but as Aubrey stared down at his plate he felt an awful conviction steal over him, and he laid down his fork, no longer hungry. A strange man and a strange woman; but he had been studying the essence of things these past weeks, and he did not think either of them had come into the world human. They had not at the core of themselves the things that humans had; their bodies seemed to have grown all the necessary organs and their faces to have been carved with the right features, but these were not the bodies and the faces they had once owned. They had been changed; and Aubrey knew of only one man in this kingdom who practiced the art of shape-changing.

"You look ill," Lilith said, her voice breaking through the wave of nausea that had caused Aubrey to grip the table with both hands. "Shall I send Arachne for some medicine? I believe my husband keeps a full complement of herbs on hand."

Assuredly he would, but Aubrey was leery of taking something Glyrenden had mixed and left behind. He shook his head. "Nothing, thank you," he said in a strangled voice. "I think perhaps I will lie down again, though."

So he did; and he forced himself to sleep. But when he awoke, the knot of nausea was still in his stomach, a little larger now. "I have imagined it," he said aloud. "I am coming down with a fever and I am imagining things." But there was no unwarranted heat in his body and he thought his mind was clear, and in his heart he knew he had stumbled on the truth.

He spent most of that day and the next one away from the house, using one of Glyrenden's smooth, well-oiled rifles to hunt for game. There were in the house, Lilith informed him, only two firearms, and Glyrenden had told her long ago to allow Aubrey free use of them. So Audrey had inspected the rifles and found them both in pristine condition, then asked Lilith which one Orion preferred to use when he hunted.

"You must ask him," she said. "I have never seen him leave the house with a gun in his hand."

But Aubrey did not ask him, because he did not want Orion to tell him that he caught game with his bare hands. He selected one rifle at random and left the house, only returning when it was too dark to see. He had missed the communal dinner, so he ate very rapidly in the kitchen by himself, and slipped away to his bedroom. Where again he forced himself to sleep, and where he woke up in the morning with the stone still lodged in his stomach.

He breakfasted early, reloaded the gun and set off at a brisk walk. They had no need of meat, for both he and Orion had been successful the day before, but Aubrey did not think he could sit quietly in that house for an entire day, not while he was haunted by such terrible thoughts. Therefore, he would hunt, or he would pretend to hunt; and Glyrenden would be back tomorrow.

He had hiked as far as the lake he had found one day with Lilith, before some of his serenity returned to him. When he made it to the clearing, he rested the rifle against a tree trunk and sat on the top of the hillock which overlooked the pastoral scene below. As before, the squirrels played games that required them to chase each other from branch to branch; the birds made colorful patterns against the washed blue sky. A deer tiptoed to the edge of the water to drink. Aubrey sat so quietly, so lost in thought, that none of the wild things there feared him or ran from his presence.

If a man could turn himself into an animal, then he could turn an animal into a man. For some reason, the logical extension of the shape-changing spells had never occurred to Aubrey. It might not be true, of course; he had no proof, and it was not the sort of thing you could ask a mage—if he had cast spells of transmogrification upon helpless beasts basically for his own amusement. But the incantations were simple enough—once you knew the makeup of body and blood and tissue—

Again, the deer at the lake lowered its head to take a cautious swallow. *I could do that,* Aubrey thought, the idea coming to him uninvited but fully formed. *I could be that deer and take that drink. I have studied him long enough.*

The thought filled him with the first true excitement he had felt for days, and he fought to keep himself calm, to truly assess his abilities. Well, he had been taught some of the spells. He had not practiced them under a master's supervision, and that was always the requirement the first time a dangerous spell was spoken; that was only common sense. He perhaps could transform himself into a stag, but could he transform himself back? Could the animal remember what the man knew and follow the same complicated processes of reason? Perhaps not; perhaps not yet. He would be foolish to try it.

But he rose to his feet anyway with his mind made up.

Quickly, he stripped himself naked, making a small pile of his clothes and laying them neatly with the rifle by the tree. Then, moving into the patch of sunlight that had evaded the screen of the leaves overhead, he dropped to his knees and placed his hands on the ground before him. He closed his eyes and remembered everything he had read in Glyrenden's books, remembered the exact placement of every muscle and bone in a deer's body, the precise weight of the antlers on its head, the length of the jaw and the hardness of the pointed hooves. He did not speak the spell aloud, because any true wizard can cast a spell in silence, and he spoke it only once.

He did not open his eyes until the changes were complete. So different did the world appear to him that at first he thought he had spoken the wrong incantation and removed himself to some entirely different wood in a kingdom far from this one. But then he saw the rifle against the tree and the pile of man's clothes beside it, although the rifle looked three times its normal size and the clothes quite unfamiliar, and he knew that he was a deer.

He glanced forward again. Yes, that was water, though he no longer saw it as a simple, pleasant gray lake. It was larger and more perfect in outline; even from here he could make out the rocks below the surface of the water and the fish swimming in a particular current. Each separate tree between him and the body of water below took on its own significance; he found himself judging the distance between them, seeing each tree as a friendly shelter in this clearing with its potential hazards. But although they were trees, and harmless, they looked different than they had before. There was no red or yellow in their leaves, no shades of difference between the browns of the aspen and the oak. In fact, there was very little color anywhere, although every outline of every object and animal in this wilderness was distinct and sharp, and he knew what each one was even though there were some he had never seen before or noticed if he had seen.

He lifted one foot daintily, the foot that had been his left hand, and he felt the peculiar ripple of muscle extend from the joint at the hoof to the low, outthrust shoulder and across his chest. He carefully laid it on the ground again and lifted the other foot; then, one by one, his hind legs. Then, even more cautiously, he moved forward, feeling the odd interplay of bone and sinew, and catching in his nostrils as he moved the keenest mix of scents he had ever encountered.

He remained a deer most of the day, moving with gradually increasing sureness up and down the hillock by the lake and around the lake itself. It was a delightful sensation, he discovered, to run with a body meant for running; the air was alive with such rich odors that merely to smell the breeze was to feast. Sounds were complex, and even from far away brought messages to him, but nothing in the forest spoke of danger. He saw other deer come up to drink, but he stayed back from them, solitary in the forest, not wanting to alarm them. They would sense his strangeness, he knew instinctively. But some day he would be able to take their form, and run with them and drink with them, and they would never know he was not one of them.

He remained a deer till nearly sunset, and then he returned to his rifle and his pile of clothes. This should have been the hard part, but it was not. Aubrey had known since he first opened his deer's eyes to see like an animal but think like a man, that he would be able to cast the spell in reverse. He had to think it through carefully, slowly, not wanting to make a mistake, but it came to his mind even more easily this time, and then he was once again a man. He was crouched on his hands and knees, naked and wild, in a slowly darkening and brilliantly colored forest, and all the smells and sounds that had been so clear all day were muffled or swept away. He shook his head once to clear it, then fell back to a sitting position and stretched his legs out before him as far as they would go.

He was a shape-changer.

When Glyrenden returned the next day, he was in such a foul mood that Orion hid from him and Arachne stayed in the kitchen, and both Lilith and Aubrey held their tongues. Aubrey had decided the day before to make no mention of his own remarkable progress, and indeed he did not speak to Glyrenden at all until breakfast the following morning.

"Your last expedition did not go well?" he asked respectfully, as Glyrenden's scowl showed no signs of disappearing.

"Well enough," the wizard shot back. "Why do you ask?"

The teaching sessions did not go smoothly that day, for Aubrey had a hard time concealing that he had already moved beyond simple exercises; and this attempt to lie made him mispronounce even the spells he knew. But his maladroitness restored to Glyrenden some of his good humor, so Aubrey felt perhaps the deception was proving useful.

"Old Cyril told me a thing or two about your cleverness before he sent you to me," Glyrenden said as they stopped to take the afternoon meal that Arachne brought into the study. "I confess, I have only once or twice seen evidence of it. But perhaps it is a slow thing to learn, eh? I have been a shape-changer so long, I cannot recall how long it took me to learn the skills."

Aubrey was piqued by the slighting reference to his ability, but he tried to hide it. "Have you had many students besides me?" he asked. "And have I been the slowest one to learn?"

Glyrenden took a swig of light ale and gave Aubrey a somewhat malicious smile. "You are the first," he said.

"Am I really? But why?"

"I have never been interested in taking students. They waste one's time and interrupt one's schedule."

"Why did you agree to take me, then?"

If anything, the smile became more malevolent. "Because Cyril convinced me that you were special." There seemed to be no answer required to that.

Aubrey was delighted to learn that Glyrenden was to leave again in two short days, and this time be gone more than a week. More time to exercise his newfound abilities. He did not say so, of course. "Perhaps someday you will take me with you," he said instead, though by now he knew Glyrenden would never invite him. By now he was glad of it.

Glyrenden laughed. "It would inconvenience me greatly to have you at my side—this time, at least. Maybe sometime in the future. If you beg me hard enough."

Aubrey forced a smile to hide his distaste. "I begged once or twice when I first came here, and you never accepted my escort. You are not moved by begging."

"Indeed, you are wrong. I enjoy it very much."

"Perhaps then, if I plead hard enough, you will teach me something new," Aubrey said, to turn the subject. "I have not been successful yet today, and I would like something fresh to practice while you are gone."

Glyrenden regarded him narrowly for a moment, and then his mouth drew back in a feral smile. "I know just the lesson," he said, and moved over to the narrow ebony desk pushed against the back wall. After a moment's debate, he picked up a small silver statuette in the shape of a nude woman with her arms stretched luxuriously above her head.

"I have a fondness for this piece," he said. "But its color no longer pleases me. Can you turn it to gold?"

Smiling, Aubrey took the figurine from Glyrenden's hands, feeling the silken metal cool and smooth against his fingers. "I can try," he said, and silently invoked the spell.

Despite his earlier failures this day, he was astonished when the silver woman did not immediately metamorphose to gold. Having learned to change the complex circuitry of his body, he had not expected to have trouble altering any mundane inert material. How had he miscued the spell? He tightened his fingers and tried the enchantment again.

Glyrenden, as usual, was talking. "A perfect woman, is she not?" he said, in his light voice. "Such detailing in the face, in the breasts—you can almost imagine the color and texture of her skin, if she were alive, if she were human. What does she reach for, with her hands lifted up like that? For the kiss of a man? For the heat of the sun? I think she just likes to feel the suppleness and elasticity of her own body. I think she has just risen from her bed, where her lover lies sleeping, and she is thinking that now, in the daytime, her body is her own again. But at night it is his, and she knows it is his—it was his the night before and will be his again this night, but for now she feels solitary and purified and free."

As always, Aubrey was distracted by the sense of Glyrenden's words, for the wizard generally indulged in strange, seductively sinister monologues when he was trying to destroy Aubrey's concentration. Yet even so, had he been alone in the room and Glyrenden nowhere nearby, Aubrey knew he would have been unable to change the silver statue to gold. He could send his mind to the simplest, deepest level of the cast metal; he could feel the molecular bindings that held one infinitesimal fragment to the other, but he could not dissolve those bindings and rearrange them. The woman resisted his alchemy. The knowledge made him furious, but he would not let Glyrenden see. Glyrenden was teaching him something—or proving a point, it was hard to tell— and only meek deference would allow Aubrey to learn which.

He set the statue back on Glyrenden's desk. "I cannot change her," he admitted. "She is impervious to my magic."

Glyrenden smiled, well-pleased. He fondled the figurine, letting her stand where Aubrey had placed her. "And yet, she is receptive to sorcery," the wizard said. "For she was not always a woman clothed in silver."

Aubrey understood then. "She has been changed already," he said.

Glyrenden nodded. His fingers still played lovingly over the curves and surfaces of the metallic body. "A beautiful piece," he said. "Carved from cherrywood dark as port. The striations of the tree made black loops around her waist and ringed her wrists with bracelets. But I stroked her breast once and found a splinter in my hand, and that was the end of that wooden girl."

Glyrenden laughed; some irony, not apparent to Aubrey, amused him. "Now who would want a woman made of wood?" he asked. "Who would embrace a dryad? Give me flesh and blood any day."

Aubrey was tired of this posturing; he wanted to know the moral. "So the silver lady," he said. "Will she be silver forever? Or might you make her gold?"

Glyrenden gave him a quick, sharp look from those lightless black eyes. "I could make her gold, if I chose," he said haughtily. "I changed her, and her shape responds to my calling. But you cannot. For you she will never alter."

So Glyrenden was proving a point after all. "Never? Can you not teach me the spells to change something that has been shaped from something else?"

"They are the same spells," Glyrenden said, "but what has been transfigured by one man cannot be modified by another. What I have converted to stone or silver or diamond will remain stone or silver or diamond, no matter how many spells you cast."

"Once, long ago, you changed a piece of the ocean to fire, and I changed it back to water," Aubrey said. "Why was that possible, while this is not?"

"Because I meant you to find the ocean in the flame. I put no baffles in my incantation."

"You are far more powerful than I am, and I realize that," Aubrey said in a level voice. "But might a stronger wizard circumvent your spells?"

"No," Glyrenden said. "Because the shape-changer's magic is incontrovertible."

Aubrey met the black eyes, keeping his own limpid and submissive, and knew that the man was lying. It scarcely mattered; Aubrey had failed to counteract Glyrenden's spell this time, and it was likely he would fail again if he tried once more. But that did not mean the magic was unalterable. It did not mean Glyrenden could, with impunity, change every last object that came within his sight. It just meant that, to defeat him, Aubrey needed to find a better wizard—or to become a better wizard himself.

Ten

IN THE MORNING, GLYRENDEN WAS GONE. TWO DAYS later, Royel Stephanis came to visit.

That morning, Aubrey and Lilith were lingering late over breakfast. Since returning from Faren Rochester's house, Aubrey had made it a point to spend as little time alone with Lilith as possible, but he could not force himself to give up those intimate morning meals. Sometimes they sat at the breakfast table until nearly noon, saying very little but loath to leave the room. This day, it was close to the hour of ten o'clock when a rusty, discordant clamor tumbled through the house.

"What in this world—" Aubrey began, starting up from his chair, although Lilith still sat serenely in hers.

"The bell. On the front porch. Someone has arrived."

Aubrey sat down again. "A visitor? But who? You never have visitors."

She shrugged, and picked up her glass of honeyed milk. "Someone for Glyrenden, most likely."

She sipped at her milk. Arachne, who was cleaning up after the meal, continued to scrub furiously at the countertops. Orion had long since left the house.

"Aren't you going to answer the door?" Aubrey asked finally.

130

"Perhaps whoever it is will go away," Lilith said. "Perhaps he has already."

Indeed, the horrendous clangor had died down and finally ceased. Aubrey wondered who could have come to seek out the wizard.

"It could have been someone from town," he said. "Glyrenden might have ordered more gowns to be made for you."

"I don't think so."

"Perhaps it was a tradesman, then, with a bill that Glyrenden forgot to pay."

"We are never dunned here."

"Well, then—"

But before Aubrey could offer further speculation, the wretched noise started up again, filling the house with its hoarse summons. Aubrey came to his feet. "A persistent someone," he said. "I'll go see who it is, shall I?"

Lilith shrugged, and Aubrey left the room. He noticed, as he stepped gingerly through the dusty front hallway, that there was no longer any sign of the footsteps he and Lilith had left there the day her gowns had arrived. In this house, traces of human habitation were silted over quickly; even the stone and brick seemed to resent their occupation and to attempt to obliterate their presence.

The massive front door was not locked, but the catch was stiff, and it took Aubrey a moment to pry it open. When he had finally managed to throw back the door, he wished he had not bothered; he wished he had stayed in the kitchen with Lilith. He had no desire to invite Royel Stephanis inside.

"My lord," Aubrey said, his words polite but his voice edged. "The master of the house is not at home. Is there something I can help you with?"

Plainly, Royel was as chagrined to see Aubrey as Aubrey was to see him. "I—that is—no, he isn't at home," the young man said, stuttering in his discomfort. "He is at the king's court. I know he is. He arrived a day or two—you see—that is, my father has sent me to court to serve the king, so I—"

"Well, then, you'd best go back there," Aubrey said unkindly.

He made as if to swing the door shut, but it was as hard to close as it was to open, and Royel moved more quickly than Aubrey expected. He was inside the disgraceful hallway before Aubrey could stop him.

"Is *she* here?" he asked quietly.

"The wizard's wife?" Aubrey asked with some emphasis. "Yes."

"She is the one I want to see."

It was not Aubrey's house; he could not deny another man entry unless Lilith or Glyrenden told him whom to turn away. He sighed inaudibly and headed toward the kitchen. "Back this way," he said over his shoulder. He heard Royel scuff along behind him through the dirt.

In the kitchen, nothing had changed. Arachne still attacked invisible stains on the wooden countertops, Lilith still sat at the table and took tiny swallows of her milk. The shape-changer's wife looked neither surprised nor annoyed when Royel tripped into view; nor did she look pleased or embarrassed or self-conscious. She did not care at all.

"My lady," Royel said, giving her an unearned courtesy title and a bow deep enough to impress a queen. "I have hoped that I could see you again."

Scowling, Aubrey dropped into the chair closest to Lilith and waved at an empty chair across from him. "Well, since you're here, you might as well sit down," he said, supremely ungracious. "Have you eaten? Are you hungry?"

Royel did not take his eyes from Lilith's face; by feel, he found a chair, pulled it out, and seated himself. "Hungry?" he repeated. "I don't—it doesn't seem that I'm hungry."

Again, Aubrey stifled a sigh. "Arachne, if we have any food left, would you serve him a plate?" he asked. Arachne's muttering grew momentarily louder, a form of protest, and then she clattered some utensils together to prepare Royel's meal.

"You are as beautiful as I remember," Royel was saying to Lilith. "I have thought about you constantly for the past few weeks. I have thought of nothing else but your white skin and green eyes."

Aubrey rose abruptly. "I have things I must do," he said. "Royel, you might remind yourself that the lady is a married woman. There are servants in the house, and I will be within call. Do not do anything to dishonor your father's name."

Lilith's eyes lifted to his when he stood. She had not said a word since Royel entered the room, and she said nothing now, although Aubrey hesitated, thinking she might. But she merely watched him for the briefest moment, then looked down at her plate again. Aubrey left the room.

As he had promised Royel, he stayed within earshot of the house for the next few hours, chopping wood and making an ineffectual effort at weeding the flower garden that circled the house. He did not, however, really expect Royel to attempt any physical declaration of passion; the boy was too innocent, for one thing, and too well-bred, for another. But Aubrey was troubled by wondering what Lilith would say or do if such a situation arose. Would she cry out for help? Struggle in the young man's arms? Grab some convenient weapon and assault her assailant in turn? Or would she shrug and submit, as she submitted to so many indignities in her life, not seeming to care who held her, who desired her, who loved her; having no respect at all for the limits of her body or the requirements of her soul?

It was nearly twilight, and Aubrey was getting hungry, when Royel emerged from the house alone. The young man glanced around as if checking for the familiar reference points of earth and sun; when he spotted Aubrey, he came over to join him. Never had Aubrey seen a face so sorrowful and disconsolate.

"She will not listen to me," the young man said without preamble. *As if,* Aubrey thought in some exasperation, *I am his confidante and his abettor; as if he expects me to commiserate.* "I tell her that I love her, and she turns away."

"What did you expect her to do?" Aubrey asked. "She has a husband."

"She does not love him."

"She shared this information with you?"

"No."

"Then what great insight told you so?"

"It is true. I am sure of it. She does not love him—she could not."

Aubrey had said much the same thing to himself many times, but he had no proof of it. "She stays with him," he said coldly. "And she has ample opportunities to leave."

"Perhaps she has nowhere else to go. But—if she could come to me—"

"Perhaps she will," Aubrey forced himself to say, "if she knows she has the choice."

For a moment Royel did not reply. He stared down at his expensively shod feet and toed the dry dirt. "I have thought of nothing else but her," he said at last, his voice low and hopeless. "Since she first walked into Faren Rochester's fortress, I have had the picture of her in my mind day and night. I cannot talk to the other women at my father's house or in the king's court—their voices sound harsh to me; their shrill laughter falls on my ears and gives me actual pain. I have spent maybe one full day in her presence, and maybe three minutes out of those hours has she met my eyes with hers, and yet the memory of her face is so clear to me that I know nothing else will move me so greatly until the day that I die. I feel drugged. I feel bewitched. I know that her husband is a sorcerer, and I wonder if he has laid a charm on me. But I would not ask him to undo the words, revoke the spell—and I would not ask him to make me forget her. Even if I cannot be with her another day in my life, I have had this much time, and it will do me—it will see me through the other blank, empty days of my life."

Aubrey absolutely could not respond to that extraordinary speech. He felt as if the young poet had found a halted, stumbling text printed in his own brain, and turned the sentiments into verse. Royel shot him a hooded look from under his thin, dark brows.

"I know," the young lord continued, a little more rapidly, "that there is something odd about her. I know she is not like other women. All my life, I have been drawn to people who were disfigured or crippled or strange. At my father's house, there was an old hunchback, a terrifying man—all the children hid from him, all the women shrieked when he came near. But he was my friend, and he taught me many things. I have been drawn to the witchwomen of villages and the peasant boys who were born simpletons though they had amazing abilities with animals. If a beggar on the road accosts me, he is sure to have six fingers or one eye blue and the other black. I know there is something in me that is out of key—that responds only to others with the same broken music. But I cannot help it. I cannot change. And I love her."

Aubrey lifted a hand and gently laid it across the boy's back. "Your love for the wild and the strange does you credit," he said softly. "You were born to be a saint, perhaps—certainly a poet. But it does you no good to love this one. You would do better not to return here."

Royel pulled away from him, a fresh surge of determination routing his momentary despair. "She does not love him," he said with conviction.

"I don't believe she loves anybody," Aubrey replied.

Royel Stephanis left at nightfall, although Aubrey felt obliged to offer him a bed, which he refused. Lilith watched him go, a dark shape against the lingering red line of sunset, but she did not seem to be sorry.

They had eaten dinner, and watched Arachne clean the kitchen, and played three games of Drain the Well before Aubrey broached the subject of the young lord's visit.

"He seems like a nice young man," was his opening gambit.

"Who?"

"Royel Stephanis. Who else would I mean?"

She shrugged.

"Do you like him?" Aubrey pursued.

"I don't dislike him," she said.

"That's not saying very much."

Her swift smile came and went. "What is it that you want me to say?" she inquired obligingly. "Just tell me, and I will say it."

"I want you to tell me what you thought of him."

"He seems like a nice young man," she replied, giving him back his own words.

Aubrey shook his head, but he could not help smiling. "He thinks he is in love with you," he said.

"So he told me."

"Did you not care about that—one way or another? Were you pleased or angry or flustered or touched?"

"No," she said.

He did not want her to love Royel Stephanis, but the cold answer disconcerted him a little. "But it means so much to him," he persisted. "Surely you could find it in your heart to be kind to him because he cares for you so greatly."

Lilith laid her cards down and let him see the skeptical, ironic look on her face. "I do not know what men mean when they say they love me," she said. "I have heard the words 'desire' and 'passion' and 'lust,' and they are just words to me. I know the word 'love' is supposed to encompass these things and more—tenderness, you would say, some kind of empathy for the object of the emotion. I feel none of these things, therefore I do not know how another feels when he says he is experiencing love. What am I supposed to say to him? It does not matter if he loves me or not."

"That is a dreadful thing to say," Aubrey said, very quietly.

"Well, it is the truth. I thought that is what you were interested in."

"You say you don't know what a man's love feels like," Aubrey said. "And yet your husband loves you."

"My husband's love," she said, "is the most suspect of all."

"So you do not care for him," Aubrey said.

"No. I do not care for him."

"Why did you marry him, then?"

She regarded him steadily and did not answer.

"And you care for nobody? In the world?"

"I told you," she said, "I do not know what the words mean."

"But," he said, very slowly, afraid to say it but wanting to know the worst, "you told me. In the coach, as we arrived at Faren Rochester's. You told me it mattered to you, whether I stayed or went. You said that. Did you not mean it?"

She did not drop her eyes, but her expression changed, became thoughtful, as if she was just now recalling her own words and deciding what they meant. Aubrey waited, utterly motionless.

"You make my life more bearable," she said at last. "I meant what I said."

It was more than he had expected. "You consider me a friend—is that it?" he asked, feeling himself breathless as he said the words.

"I have not had much experience with friendship, either," she said. "Is that what you are? A friend?"

"I care what happens to you—I would do what I could to help you," he said, stammering a little. As bad as Royel Stephanis, but more adept at guile. "If there is something you would have me do, ask me—"

"I can think of nothing you can do for me," she said curtly. There was silence between them for a moment. Then she said, as if the words surprised her even more than they surprised him, "But I thank you for the offer."

Perhaps it was because of Royel Stephanis' impassioned words, or perhaps it was because the air was so fine the next morning; for whatever reason, Aubrey could not bring himself to leave Lilith alone at the breakfast table the following day.

"I'm restless and tired of my own company," he said. "Would you walk with me in the woods today? We have not gone exploring together for weeks."

"I would be glad to," she said, rising at once to her feet. It was the first time he had ever heard her claim to feel any emotion at all.

So they spent the whole day together, strolling the green pathways of the forest. They said very little, but their silence was companionable. Lilith, when questioned, proved to know the name of every bush and tree that grew together in disorganized fashion throughout the length and breadth of the woods, and she named each one for Aubrey as they passed. About wildflowers, however, she was strangely ignorant, and she had no interest in the names of the birds or the habits of the foxes or the formations of the clouds. Aubrey told her what he knew, but he did not flatter himself that she bothered to remember his lecture.

He was afraid to spend another day alone in her company, for that day had been, without exception, the most pleasant day of his life. He did not know what to do; he was sure his heart would break. He could not stay, he could not go, and he did not believe that if he asked her, Lilith would come away with him. It was not that she harbored any affection for Glyrenden. Oh, no. She had made her detestation of her husband plain enough—and yet, she seemed strangely unwilling to forsake him. Any other unhappy wife, abandoned for days at a time in a remote house on the far reaches of civilization, would have surprised her husband with an empty house one day when he came back from his wandering; but Lilith stayed. And never spoke of leaving.

The same was true of the other inmates of the house, a fact that puzzled Aubrey almost as much, and worried him as well. For Orion was clearly afraid of the wizard; he cowered when Glyrenden came too close, and never stayed in any room with him longer than was strictly necessary. Arachne seemed to have no emotions of any kind, but she kept herself always more than arm's length from the shape-changer, and ducked her head nearer to her chest any time he walked into a room. So they had no love for him, and as far as Aubrey could tell, he paid them no wage. So why did they stay?

Because they want him to change them back.

The thought came to Aubrey late that night, far past midnight, as he lay sleeplessly listening to a storm crashing through the forest. It clawed at his closed shutter and raged across the eaves and turrets, and it made him restless enough to stand, light his candle and begin pacing his uneven floor. Lately, it took magic to make him sleep through the night, and even in his dreams his stomach held a stone in it, heavier each day and darker in color.

They want him to change them back.

Surely that could not be true; surely his wild suspicions were lunatic, unfounded. A strange man and a strange woman, who had been made briefly beautiful with magic; why did he believe they had ever been anything other than what they were now?

But the stone rocked and turned in his stomach. *They want him to change them back.*

Aubrey spent the next three days alone in the forest, undergoing a variety of transformations. He became a deer again, and then a hawk, and he caught one night's supper in that winged and taloned form. He made himself a cougar, sleek and deadly; an owl, wide-eyed and impassive; a fish, mindlessly joyous. He thought of Orion and made himself into a bear, slow-witted but cunning; he thought of Arachne, and changed himself into a spider, quick and industrious. That last transformation was the most difficult of all and the hardest to return from. He came back to his own shape nauseous and sweating. The spider was too far removed from the human shape to allow for easy interrelation, but at least the experiment had been valuable; it had answered that question and stretched his ability. The next day he made himself a moth and an ant and a firefly, and that day it was easier.

He became, in a few short days, so skilled that he could move from one form to another without becoming a man in between, although he could not do it rapidly. He made himself a dove, a cardinal and a jay; a squirrel, a weasel and a beaver; a wolf, a hound and a fox. He made himself every kind of animal he could think of; he was within a very few days almost every species known to the kingdom, but none of them felt familiar to him. Not one of them reminded him of Lilith, and the stone in his stomach grew larger.

For he was in love with her and she would break his heart; she had not been born a woman but even now he did not know what she was.

• • •

It was then that Aubrey decided he needed to visit Faren Rochester's home again, to talk with the lord's sorcerer.

"I'll be gone a day or two," he told Lilith.

She did not ask where he was going; did not care, probably. "What shall I tell Glyrenden if he returns before you do?" she asked.

"I don't think he will," Aubrey replied. "If he does, say you have no notion where I am."

He had walked half a mile along the road toward Rochester's before he paused and began to ready himself for travel. Having given this a good deal of thought in the past few days, he was prepared. He took off his clothes, the thinnest ones he owned, and carefully folded them into a flat, lightweight pack. He slipped the pack over his shoulders, tying it carefully under his arms and around his waist till it did not bind anywhere. Once it was in place, he spoke the spellwords, and melted into wolf shape.

He took a few tentative steps, and then tried a light run, but the pack was still inconvenient. He turned himself to a man and tried again, this time tying the bundle so that it lay against his chest. Back in wolf shape, he trotted forward again, his stride settling into an easy lope as the ropes of the pack grew more familiar.

The colorless miles flashed by; the acres of forest that he had found so uninspiring on his first trip this way now seemed thick with noise and incident and odor. He stopped for water at a running stream. When he was hungry, he caught an indolent rabbit and ate it raw. His mind turned on the most immediate problems: the presence of game, the sensation of thirst, the occasional whisper of danger. Toward nightfall, he heard men's voices far ahead and caught the pungent whiff of their campfire. He altered his course and ran invisibly around them.

When he tired, he turned himself into a man again, and slept. He would have liked to remain in animal form, but it was still too new to him; he could not be sure his borrowed instincts would keep him safe in the night. It seemed more sensible to sleep as a man, to face only the dangers a man might face, so that if he woke in peril he could respond in the ways with which he was most familiar.

He rose early the next morning, resumed his wolf appearance, and raced on through the forest. It was still a few hours before noon when he arrived on Faren Rochester's land and came to a halt. His legs grew thicker and his eyes remembered color; he felt his skin turn smooth and thin. He changed back into a man.

He did not want to present himself at the door. Faren Rochester seemed like the sort who would wonder why one wizard was seeking the counsel of another, and Aubrey did not particularly feel like explaining. So he caught a morning breeze and endowed it with a message, and sent it skirling into the magician's chamber. Then he dressed himself and smoothed down his hair, hoping he did not present a ragged appearance. He felt as if a trace of wildness lingered somewhere in the slant of his eyes or the fierceness of his posture; the longer he stayed a wolf, the more difficult it would be to become wholly human again.

Sirrit did not make him wait long, but came strolling through the forest within an hour. He picked his way through the undergrowth with the aid of a silver and ebony cane, and he navigated without circuit to the glade Aubrey had chosen.

"Good morning," the elder wizard greeted the younger, nodding as casually as if they were in the habit of meeting for conferences in the woods. "You're traveling some distance from home."

"I felt the need for company," Aubrey said with a quick, cursory smile.

Sirrit glanced around, but Aubrey was sure it was a deliberate charade. "Where's your horse?"

"I came on foot."

Sirrit glanced down to see Aubrey's feet covered only in thin woolen socks; his boots had been too heavy to carry in his pack. "Not on those feet, I'll wager," the wizard said dryly.

"No," Aubrey said. "I have been practicing my newest skills."

"Ah." Sirrit pointed with his cane, and led Aubrey to the trunk of a mammoth fallen tree. They both sat. "So Glyrenden is in fact teaching you to be a shape-changer."

"That is what I came to him to learn."

"Well, he is the master. But he has not been overfond of taking students, in the past."

"I wonder why he took me, then."

Sirrit gave him a sidelong look and seemed to consider. "Glyrenden believes in getting to know his enemy."

"His enemy? I was never that," Aubrey said—and then fell silent. For he knew that was, now at least, a lie.

"Some years ago," Sirrit said, settling himself more comfortably on the log, "we were better friends. Glyrenden, and Cyril and I, and men whose names you would not know if I told them. Cyril, who could always forecast better than any of us, took his scrying crystal and told us each our futures. I was to grow old and fat in some lord's service, Cyril was to win respect and acclaim, Mintele was to travel to foreign lands to battle some ancient magical creature. Prophecies like that. Glyrenden was told that his fate lay in the hands of a young magician whose name he would recognize when he heard it."

"His fate," Aubrey repeated. "What does that mean?"

Sirrit shrugged. "Who knows? Was this young man to save Glyrenden's life or make his reputation or utterly destroy him? Cyril could not be more specific." Sirrit gave Aubrey another sideways glance. "But I have to believe your name sounded familiar to Glyrenden, and so he took you on when you applied."

"It was Cyril's idea that I go to Glyrenden," Aubrey said. "He would not teach me the shape-changing spells himself."

"But Glyrenden has shared them with you?"

"Some of them. Some I have puzzled out on my own. Some of them—" Aubrey hesitated, shrugged and then burst out: "Sirrit, I am learning some things I wish I had never known."

"Knowledge is always double-edged," the sorcerer replied.

"That cannot be true."

"Believe it," Sirrit said. "There is not a spell you will learn from now until you die that cannot be misused or misdirected."

"I have learned the most barbarous spell there is," Aubrey said, very low.

"And that is?"

"How to create a human being from something that was not human at all."

Sirrit planted his cane between his feet and rested his clasped hands on its silver handle. "Oh," he said, "that is not so barbaric."

Aubrey turned shocked eyes to him. "How can you say that? You were the one who lectured me about the existence of the universal soul—"

Sirrit held up one hand to silence him. "Very well. Barbaric, then, but not surprising. The oldest urge in the range of human desires is to create another being in a familiar image. To create another being to love. That is why you were born, why I was born—why any of us is alive today and traveling from city to city—because the human drive to procreate is as strong as the drive to live."

"Yes—but—that is a natural act, an inevitable progression of the race. But to make something—a being, a man or a woman—from material that was something else—"

Sirrit shrugged. "Wizards take shortcuts," he said. "And they like to improve upon the imperfect human process."

"It is outrageous!"

"No doubt, but it's not amazing," Sirrit said. "The second-strongest human urge is to find something helpless and control it."

"That's not true!" Aubrey said hotly.

Sirrit regarded him for a moment with a half-smile. "Well, perhaps you're right," he conceded. "But for some men it is an irresistible urge."

Aubrey stared at him. If this man was as unprincipled as Glyrenden, if the whole race of wizards was addicted to such games of power, then he had cast his last spell; he could not bear to practice magic another day. "Have you ever," he asked, his voice almost a whisper, "called forth such a creature? Done such a thing?"

"This was not a branch of magic that appealed to me," Sirrit said dryly. "I never learned the spells."

Aubrey felt a rush of relief; he knew it colored his face rosy.

"Cyril knows them but he will not use them, nor will many of the other great sorcerers. But you have learned them," Sirrit said softly. "And having learned them, you cannot unlearn them. That is one of the other dark prices of knowledge."

"I did not come here to ask you to teach me how to forget," Aubrey said.

"Why, then?"

"To ask you how to undo another magician's spell."

There was a long silence. "The easiest way," Sirrit said, "is to kill him."

"That is not the way I would choose."

"No, and it is not always effective, either," Sirrit said with a certain amount of regret. "Usually it is! I was in Cannewold when the sorcerer Talvis died, and I saw with my own eyes the ocean surge through the dams he had constructed to keep the city safe. I saw the houses fall to the blue hunger of the waves, and I saw sea foam swirl around the high spire of the viceroy's castle. A thousand men perished in that flood, and all because the magic died with the man."

"But when Soetan died, the roses still bloomed on Virris Mountain, and it was his spell that had turned that barren earth fruitful," Aubrey said. "And no wizard, not you nor Cyril nor Talvis himself, was able to reverse the spell that Soetan laid on King Reginald, and so the man finished his days blind and mute."

"Well, Soetan was a man of exceptional gifts," Sirrit said. "And it is hard indeed to break a spell when a powerful wizard does not want it to be circumvented."

"How is it done, then?" Aubrey said. "Because I must know."

"You have to be a better wizard," Sirrit said simply.

Aubrey just looked at him.

"There is more, of course," the old sorcerer continued. "You must love the thing itself, the thing that you are restoring—not the thing that it has become, which is sometimes more beautiful and more useful than the thing it was, but the thing that it was brought into the world to be. The reason none of us could return King Reginald to his former state was that none of us, really, liked him, and we had all rather preferred the world when he could not watch our doings or comment upon them. None of us would have visited his infirmities upon him, I believe, but we couldn't quite bring ourselves to correct his problems."

"How can you love something you have never seen in its primeval state?" Aubrey asked. He had grown chilly at the wizard's words; he knew what it was to prefer the alteration to the original.

"That's the first unanswerable question," Sirrit said. "There is another."

Aubrey looked over with dread. "What?"

"When you release something from the grip of magic, or when you reverse magic, you put that person or that object at tremendous risk. Magic changes people—things—it sometimes makes them unfit to exist on their own. How do you keep from destroying the very thing you are trying to restore?"

"How?" Aubrey demanded.

Sirrit shook his head. "I don't know. No one knows. Magic, my friend, is even more capricious than love. Only you know how much your own is to be trusted."

"My own magic, or my own love?" Aubrey said, rising to his feet. He felt shaky, a little dizzy. He wished he could believe it was the shape-changing that had so unnerved him, but he knew it was the conversation.

"Both," said Sirrit. "Either."

Eleven

AUBREY WAS BACK AT GLYRENDEN'S HOUSE EARLY THE next morning, preceding the master of the house only by a matter of hours. But even had Aubrey been absent when Glyrenden returned, the wizard probably would not have noticed: He brought company with him, and all his attention was for her.

His new companion was a shy and frightened young girl Glyrenden called his niece. She was very small and very brown, with large liquid eyes and a dappling of freckles over her nose. She moved with a startled fluidity that was beautiful to watch. The slightest noise made her jump from her chair or tense in her tracks. As she moved from room to room she made her way cautiously from chair to sofa to table, as if taking shelter behind each piece before moving forward again. Glyrenden said she did not know their country's language, but Aubrey suspected she had no human speech at all.

"We shall call her Eve," Glyrenden said fondly, running his cold, thin hand lovingly down the silky river of her hair. "Is that not a lovely name, my pet?"

She shivered under his touch but did not move away. Indeed, at all times she fixed her eyes on his face with a strange beseeching intensity whether he was near her or across the room; she never missed a single move he

150

made. For his part, Glyrenden was quite besotted with her. He loved to sit by the girl, holding her small hand in his and stroking her hair back from her face, or dropping his hands to her shoulders and giving them a slight squeeze.

"Is she not lovely?" he murmured to Aubrey, or to Lilith, or to whoever was in the room. "Is she not perfect, in fact?"

It was obvious she was not his niece, but whether or not she was his lover, Aubrey was not able to determine. She looked to be barely out of her early teens, undeveloped and girlish, but even her slight charms were irresistible to the shape-changer. He even neglected to pay his usual cloying court to Lilith while Eve was in the house; all his sinister attention was focused on the girl.

What Lilith thought about the introduction of Eve to this household was impossible to guess. She treated the girl as she treated everyone else, with a cool indifference that was neither welcoming nor hostile. If she felt any jealousy—or compassion—it did not show. She simply did not care.

As for Aubrey, he walked around the house as a man inflicted with the influenza, his stomach in perpetual torment and the weight slowly dropping from his body.

From the time that Glyrenden returned with Eve, all lessons halted. The wizard was too taken with his young prize to waste time with a troublesome student, and Aubrey was too sick to ask for the shape-changer's attention. Although this was the busy season at the king's court, Glyrenden made no mention of leaving again soon; there was no way to know how long he would be at home this time.

So for several weeks they lived in a strange, uneasy state of idleness, the two men and the four changed things, and each of them filled the days as best they could. Arachne cleaned and cooked and kept to herself; Orion hunted by day and slept noisily in the evenings. Lilith and Aubrey played cards endlessly, match after match of picquet and whist and cribbage, till even the unmarked decks became familiar and predictable. And Glyrenden gloated over his newest possession.

It was by sheerest accident that Aubrey and Glyrenden came face to face one afternoon in the study where they had once practiced exercises and which now they seldom used at all. Aubrey was searching for a book Glyrenden had once lent him; the older wizard was looking up some wayward piece of knowledge. No one else was present.

"Still studying, my pet?" Glyrenden asked him, with that half-mocking smile that Aubrey had finally realized was really a sneer. "And have you learned much of any worth since I have neglected you so shamefully of late?"

"I have taught myself what I could," Aubrey replied. "But I have rarely found my own invention good enough to equal a tutor's guidance."

"No—how should you, indeed? It is a pity I have been gone so much, I know."

Aubrey took a deep breath. "Perhaps it is time I left you . . ." he said slowly. "If you have no time to teach me—if I am in your way—"

Glyrenden smiled widely, his expression so wicked that Aubrey felt the very bones in his body shrink inward. "Do not pretend you will ever leave me," he drawled. "You will stay with me months and weeks and years. You want so many of the things that I already have."

Aubrey turned cold. What, besides his knowledge, did Glyrenden suspect that he coveted? "Why did you take me on as a pupil, Glyrenden?" he asked, for the first time using the wizard's name as an equal would. "Merely from fear that I was really as good as Cyril said I was?"

Glyrenden was still smiling. "It is a wise man who learns his antagonist young," he replied.

"If you consider me an adversary, why teach me the spells at all?"

"Half the spells," Glyrenden murmured.

Aubrey laughed shortly. "You think to leave me hungry," he said. "But you have gained no power over me by treating me in such a way."

"Have I not? Why are you still here then, Aubrey, my pet, my lamb? What holds you here, if it is not desire?" His smile, impossibly, widened. "Or is it fear?"

"I begin to think it is hatred, Glyrenden," he replied quietly.

"Ah," the sorcerer breathed. "Then you have learned something from me after all."

That was the last private conversation that passed between the wizard and his apprentice for the next fortnight. The mood at the house grew more strained as the days passed; this was the longest period of time Glyrenden had spent at his own house since Aubrey first took up residence there. Everyone waited, with an unvoiced hope, for the day some new commission would take the wizard away again; but the days passed, and no such commission came.

Aubrey and Lilith had ceased playing cards except in the evenings. Now they spent much of their day walking, careless of what construction Glyrenden might put on their obvious preference for each other's company. During those hikes, in the bracing autumn air, Aubrey almost managed to be happy, almost managed to overlook the stone in his stomach and the continual, tortured circling of his thoughts. He could not persuade himself that Lilith felt any warmer feelings for him than mere liking, but since she did not even like anyone else, that was almost enough for him.

During those weeks, they talked only once about Eve, whom they had come across that afternoon at the border of the woods. They had found her with her mouth bloodied and her large brown eyes red with tears. Aubrey had crouched beside her, though she drew away in alarm, and healed as best he could the scrapes and bruises on her arms and legs. She would not answer his gentle questions, but as soon as he finished his ministrations, she struggled to her feet and ran back toward the house. The two of them watched her go, then slowly resumed their walk toward the clearing in the forest.

"Did Glyrenden beat her?" Aubrey asked at last.

Lilith shook her head. "I doubt it. His abuses seldom run that way."

"Then what happened?"

Lilith shrugged. "I don't know. Probably she climbed the highest tree she could find and jumped from it, but the fall did not kill her."

Aubrey was horrified. "Was she trying to kill herself?"

"It would not surprise me."

Now he looked at Lilith with a fear that he knew would never leave him again as long as Glyrenden was alive. "Have you ever tried to kill yourself? Since he brought you to this house?"

She made a disinterested gesture with her hand. "Once, I did. I was not successful. Glyrenden's women are proof against death."

"Why do you stay with him?" he whispered, though he knew the answer. "Why do you not run away?"

She looked over at him and suddenly the indifference was gone from her. Beneath her unemotional mask he sensed a longing so great that his own love for her was a paltry thing beside it. "Because only he can give me the one thing I want."

He shook his head. "He will never give it to you."

"I know. But I will get it nowhere else in this kingdom." They had arrived at the clearing that had become, of every place in this entire forest, their place especially, and she asked him, "Why do you stay? Merely because you want to learn his terrible spells?"

He shook his head again, and spoke the truth with some desperation. "I stay because I cannot leave you," he said. "I love you. Not even Glyrenden's evil is enough to drive me away."

The clean lines of her face softened slightly, but she shook her head in denial. "I have told you before what I think of the love of men," she said. "I do not know what to do with it when it is offered to me, and I have none to offer in return. I thought you understood."

"I understood," he said. "But it did not change me. Do not send me away as you sent away Royel Stephanis."

He saw her lips shape themselves to ask, Who? but then she remembered. "I would not wish you to go just because you love me," she said.

He had no answer for that, but the cool reply strangely enough did not discourage him. He thought, if anything, she was faintly pleased by his declaration; but he knew better than to press his suit.

Instead, during the long walk home, he asked her the question he had wanted to ask for so long. He did not know how she would react to the inquiry, so he approached it obliquely, with another question.

"Will she be all right, do you think?" he said first.

"Will who be all right?" Lilith asked.

"Eve."

Lilith shrugged. "She will not be happy. She will not be tame. I don't think she will die of him, but I can't be sure. It looks as though she will survive the day, at any rate."

Aubrey looked away from her to study the overgrown path before them, which—with their constant traveling—had come to resemble a trail again. "She is a doe, of course," he said calmly, "or a fawn, rather. Very young. And I have learned the truth about Arachne and Orion, or I think I have. But you are still a mystery. I have studied the shapes of all the animals in the kingdom and not one of them reminds me of you. What is it that you really are?"

For a moment she did not answer, and he thought she might not tell him—or, even more unlikely, did not know. Then she said, and her voice was dreamy, "In all this kingdom, there is only one place that I love and one place that I would consider beautiful. It is called the King's Grove, and in it is planted one of every kind of tree that grows. No man is allowed to hunt there, no gardener to prune, and when the wind comes through on a summer evening the singing of the mingled leaves is a chorus so sweet that even the birds pause to listen. The scent of cedar blends with the fragrance of the blossoms on the fruit trees, and the white of the birch is no more beautiful than the heavy auburn of the elm. When the leaves are silent, there is no sound at all, and the only word is the echo of the name for peace."

And then he knew. He looked at her again and saw

not the smooth brown hair and the coarse gray gown, but a long full shape, limber and graceful and arched against the sun. "A willow," he said.

"Yes," she replied.

Two days later, early in the morning, Aubrey was awakened by an urgent knocking at his bedroom door. "Just a minute!" he called out, dragging himself from his bed and pulling on a threadbare robe. He could not recall a time during the months he had stayed in this house that someone had summoned him early from bed.

Lilith stood outside the door, already dressed in one of her gray gowns. "Come quickly," she said. He had rarely seen her so stirred up; a wash of color accentuated the line of her cheekbones.

"What is it?" he demanded, following her down the steep steps.

"Eve," she replied. "Hurry."

They found the young girl in the last place Aubrey would have expected—Glyrenden's study. She lay on the floor, curled tightly in upon herself, moaning piteously. Her glossy hair was spread in tangled disarray over the stone floor; her nightdress was torn and twisted around her body. Arachne stood to one side of her, whispering under her breath. The room smelled unpleasantly of vomit—and something else even more malevolent.

Aubrey dropped instantly beside the girl. "What happened?" he asked.

"I don't know. Arachne found her a few minutes ago and came to get me."

Aubrey touched the colorless face, then ran his fingers lightly down from the girl's throat to her abdomen. "Poison," he said grimly. "One of Glyrenden's mixtures, no doubt."

"Can you help her?" Lilith asked.

"I don't know. It depends on what she's taken." He looked up at her. "Where's Glyrenden?"

She gestured. "Gone. In the middle of the night. I don't know where or for how long."

Aubrey nodded and rose to his feet. "Heat some milk," he directed Arachne. "And some water. We'll want to clean her up."

Lilith left with Arachne. Aubrey prowled the magician's study, looking for clues. They were not hard to find. Eve had apparently crept down to the magician's room as soon as he left, and put together a mixture of whatever potions were easiest to hand. She had left the jars standing open on the table, some of their contents spilled nearby. Aubrey tasted and identified each one: rue, belladonna, curare, and a handful of ensorcelled herbs, given more potency by magic. Any one of these would have been enough to kill the girl, but she had mixed too well—they had reacted against each other and made her so ill she could not keep them in her body. Her eagerness to die had no doubt saved her life.

Nonetheless, some of the toxin was still seething through her blood; her continued pain made that obvious. Glyrenden was not the kind of man to accidentally drink his own poisons, nor to administer them and then regret, so he had not bothered to brew antidotes for any of the deadly potions on his shelves. Aubrey worked quickly, combining ingredients for the cures he knew, guessing at the ones he didn't.

Arachne entered behind him, carrying a kettle of hot milk. "Set it there," Aubrey said. "And I'll need a clean glass, and a spoon—yes, thank you."

Lilith had returned at Arachne's heels, bringing towels and a pail of water. She had a clean muslin night-gown thrown over one shoulder.

"Will she be ill again?" the wizard's wife asked practically. "I don't want to ruin another nightdress."

"No, I don't think so," Aubrey said. "I think the chemicals have already been absorbed too far into her system. Now we have to counteract them, not expel them."

Lilith nodded and knelt at the girl's side. Aubrey, mixing the hot milk into his desperate concoction, spared a moment to watch Lilith work. As he might have expected, she was neither distressed nor repulsed by the sick and filthy girl; she took the brown head onto her lap and began wiping away the vomit and spittle. What surprised Aubrey was her gentleness, what he would even call tenderness if he did not know better. Eve cried out once sharply, when Lilith began to unbutton the collar of her nightgown.

"Ssh," Lilith said, her voice almost a croon. "Ssh, now. You will be all right. You'll see. It is not as bad as you think."

No, it's worse, Aubrey thought, turning back to his stirring. He had never known Lilith to lie before, even to offer comfort. In fact, he had never known Lilith to offer comfort. He felt a small, irrational chill shiver at the base of his neck, and he shook his head to dispel it.

By the time Aubrey's potion was mixed, Lilith had cleaned and changed the girl, even combing out the knotted masses of her hair. Aubrey knelt down and handed Lilith the glass of doctored milk.

"I'll hold her up," he said, taking Eve into his arms and raising her against his shoulder. "You help her drink."

Eve resisted, but they managed to pour most of the

drugged milk down her throat. She still had not opened her eyes, and she did not seem to be conscious, but she thrashed in Aubrey's arms and uttered intermittent cries of horror. But the potion had its quick effect. Shortly after she swallowed it, she calmed a little. Her body relaxed and she seemed to tumble down the precipice of sleep.

"Now what will happen?" Lilith asked.

"Now I don't know," Aubrey said. "I am only guessing with all of this."

"Can we move her somewhere more comfortable?"

"Yes."

Aubrey rose with Eve in his arms and carried her back to the kitchen. It was the warmest room in the house, the place where they could all hover round and watch her. Orion had made up a bed for her on a cot by the stove, and Aubrey laid her there gently. She turned to her side and did not move again.

"Sick," Orion said.

"Very sick," Aubrey agreed. "But we hope she will get better."

"We should have Arachne clean the study," Lilith said. "Before he gets home."

"We'd best do it ourselves," Aubrey said. "I would not like to leave any signs of Eve's trespassing."

So they got more buckets of water and a handful of rags and returned to the sour-smelling study. They had worked about half an hour in silence when Lilith spoke.

"What will happen to her?"

"She will be sick a day or two, and she will have to eat easy things, like soup and bread. And then she should be all right."

Lilith looked over at Aubrey sorrowfully. She stood across the room from him, the very picture of a domestic servant—her dark hair piled on her head, her gray skirt hitched up, a wet rag wrapped around both hands. And yet she did not look humble or ridiculous to Aubrey.

"No," she said. "What will happen to her, Aubrey? While she continues to live in this house?"

He felt that stone in his stomach grow heavier. "What will happen to any of you?" he asked in turn.

Lilith gestured and laid aside her cloth. "For the rest of us, it does not matter so much," she said. "Arachne and Orion he does not trouble. They were not formed for his pleasure, merely for his amusement. He created them but he leaves them alone."

"And for you? How can you say it does not matter?"

She shrugged. "It is not the same," she said. "I have no instinctual terror at the touch of a man's hand. I was not born hating and distrusting men—I was brought into the world with no thought of them at all. But for her it is different. It is worse. And she is so much younger. And I have had time to grow used to him."

"What are you saying?" he said. "What are you asking me to do?"

She shook her head. "There is nothing you can do," she said. "I know that. Or you would."

And his stomach lurched again. He carefully set down the tiny glass jar he had been wiping clean; it was too heavy for him to hold. "I would," he said. "I would."

She sighed and sat down where she had stood, appearing, for the first time since he had known her, weary, discouraged and sad. Human. "Perhaps," she said slowly, "we should have let her die."

"She probably would not have died with the toxins she had taken. She just would have suffered longer before she recovered."

"Then perhaps you should have given her the drugs

she wanted instead of the drugs that would allow her to heal."

He stepped around the damp places where he had mopped, and settled himself beside Lilith on the floor. "I have never killed a human being," he said slowly. "I don't know if I could do it."

"She has the shape of a woman, but she is not a woman. You would kill a deer for food."

"For food," he agreed. "But not—not—" He gestured, unable to complete the sentence.

"If you came across a doe wounded in the woods, and you could not save her, you would kill her," Lilith said swiftly. "It is the same thing."

"It may be the same thing," he said, "but I cannot give her the potions that will let her die." He was silent a moment, thinking.

"I came to magic," he said at last, "with joy. I thought it was a splendid thing to take the well of power that I found within me and shape it to marvelous uses. I learned to call up wind and control fire, to draw flowers from barren soil and divert rain to the desert. I learned to exorcise madness from men's brains and to banish illness from their blood. I can create illusions, I can make a scrying crystal give me visions that are literal, that are true. And everything I learned made me happy—made others happy. And that is what I learned magic for.

"But magic, I have discovered, it like any skill. It is not inherently good in itself. And some of it—yes, some of it *is* inherently evil. There are wicked spells, savage spells, enchantments that are so black that even to know them withers the heart just a little, taints the soul. And yet to be a great magician, to be a sorcerer of any ability or renown, those spells must be learned as well. For if a magician does not know them, they can be used against him—and what is magic, after all, but a man's power to change the world while it is incapable of changing him?

"I came to magic with joy," he repeated, "but even as it turns joyless in my hands, I cannot look away from it. I must know it all, its breadth and its depth and its darkness. I am hungry for it, even as it sickens me. I am addicted to it."

"There is no hope for any of us, then," Lilith said quietly, "if someone like you can be corrupted."

He put out his hand and lifted her chin. Her eyes stared back at his unwaveringly. He had never seen her face so sad. "No," he said gently, "let me finish. I must have knowledge, but I do not have to use it. Cyril taught me that a long time ago. There were spells that he knew, that he would not use, that he would not even teach. He was like a farmer who owned a cache of weapons and kept them buried in the ground. I am that kind of person as well. Glyrenden has taught me how to change my shape, but I have always come back as the man I was before."

"Leave us now, then," she whispered, "before he changes you as he has changed us all."

"I have told you already," he said, bending forward, "why I cannot leave."

He kissed her lightly, a feather kiss, feeling the shape of her mouth long and distinct against his own. She neither responded nor pulled away. When he lifted his head, she was watching him, her face puzzled and her eyes questioning.

"I love you," he added, in case she did not remember. "If you wanted to be a woman, I would try to make you love me in return."

She came slowly to her feet, staring down at him. "But I do not want to be a woman," she said.

"I know," he said.

He was not surprised when she left the room without speaking again. He spent the rest of the day cleaning Glyrenden's study by himself.

Twelve

EVE WAS BETTER THE NEXT DAY AND GLYRENDEN HAD NOT returned. "Two good omens," Aubrey observed over breakfast. "I am not a superstitious man, but I shall not overlook the portents."

Lilith glanced at him expressionlessly. It was probably his imagination, but she seemed wary of him this morning, as she had over dinner last night. "You speak in riddles," she said.

"I have something I want to try," he said. "This might be a good day. I don't know when I'll be back."

She nodded and did not ask him where he was going or what he planned. From her husband she had learned that few men appreciate curiosity; or perhaps she had never been curious to begin with. Aubrey accepted a packet of food from Arachne and set out well before noon.

He walked far and fast, deep into the forest, miles from the glade where he had first learned to be a shape-changer. For this particular exercise, he wanted to be removed from any familiar place, any clearing or acre that held the faint but unmistakable imprint of man.

It was noon before he stopped. He was three miles from the nearest pathway that branched off the main road; he had broken his way through heavy undergrowth

165

for the last six hundred yards, and he had come upon the smallest open clearing in the woods. Here, the close fraternity of trees was broken, and sunlight splashed down to the greedy grass beneath the thick interweave of branches. Perhaps, decades ago, another oak or elm had stood here shoulder to shoulder with its neighbors. Now there was an empty circle here in the heart of the forest, and Aubrey stood there, getting his bearings.

To change something back, Sirrit had said, you must love the thing it had been before. Aubrey touched the rough bark of the tree closest to him, and thought about that.

A tree is composed of the elements, Sirrit had said: earth, air, water, fire. A man, on the other hand, is only air and water.

Aubrey lifted his face to the sun, deliberately analyzing the feel of its heat across his bones, the sickle of his cheek, the tight curve of his chin. Sirrit had been wrong about that. A man is air and water, but he is also fire as a tree is fire, taking his primordial spark from the distant, essential conflagration of the sun.

And is he earth, too? Aubrey wondered. Man ate the fruits of the earth, giving him some alliance. Might he skip that intermediate step, and teach himself to take his sustenance directly from the rich, unadulterated soil?

Quickly, Aubrey bent to strip off his boots and his woolen socks; then he unlaced, unbuckled and discarded every last item of his clothing. It was possible, he knew (he had been practicing), to change shapes and not be troubled by garments he had neglected to remove. But for this transformation he wanted nothing in his way.

He dug his bare feet into the black soil, critically noting its composition. Generations of leaves, bits of bark, airborne debris, the remains of animals long dead;

deeper still, the elemental compounds—nitrogen, nickel, copper, iron. He burrowed farther, feeling the striated layers of the earth ringing his ankles and his calves, touching, far beneath the placid surface of the ground, the secret, quick-running table of water.

He raised his hands above his head, stretching his arms as high as they would go, and then higher, reaching for the sun itself. He spread his fingers, multiplying the surfaces upon which the sun could fall, till he offered twenty fingers, fifty, a hundred, an uncounted number, flat and shiny and marbled with heliotropic veins. He felt the wind shake through him and set him to dancing through his shoulders and his elbows; but his torso remained stable, firm, rooted in the earth.

He felt the slow drag of chemicals through the entire length of his body, pulled from the soil around his toes, up through the arteries of his legs, past his heart, through his shoulder blades, winding across his thin forearms, and bursting out through the very tips of his fingers in a bright, joyous explosion. He could not see shapes or colors, yet he was aware when the light faded, to be replaced by a blackness that was complete but unalarming. Again, the light, growing slowly, until there was nothing but light, simple and sufficient; then a gradual descent again into the serene, uncomplicated night.

If his body had a pulse, it had slowed to this lazy, diurnal rhythm; the valves of his heart opened at dawn and closed again at sunset. If he breathed, it was through every pore of his body, and not through his useless, imprisoned lungs. He was not conscious of sleeping or being awake, but merely of existing; and the existence was composed of light and quiet ecstasy.

It was five days before he remembered what he really was, and remembered how to become that again. The transformation was slow, reluctant and disorienting; he lay on the ground a long time as he reaccustomed himself to the sensation of blood skittering across his bones. Later, hiking back through the forest, he felt as uncoordinated and clumsy as a child first learning to walk. His breath came fast and short, and his heart troubled him with its insistent pounding. He paused once to rest, leaning his back against a massive oak, and he found his body almost unconsciously molding itself to the contours of that well-remembered shape. He forced himself to stand upright again, quickly, and resumed walking back toward the haunts of men.

He had come to love trees too well, he thought, in a few short days. Or perhaps he had already loved them for longer than he knew.

By noon, his own body no longer felt strange to him, and he strode along at a rapid pace. As always when he had mastered some new and difficult skill, he was pleased with himself, and his pleasure colored his entire outlook. The depression that had hovered over him lifted perceptibly; he actually whistled a little as he walked. He found that he was hungry, a rare state these days, so he stopped to make a midday meal out of the rations he had brought with him five days ago. The bread was stale and the dried meat very tough. He would look for fruit and other edibles as he continued through the forest.

He was back on the main road, but still a good two hours from Glyrenden's, when he spotted a fellow wanderer heading his way. "Hulloa there!" he called out, waving his arm. In his present mood of exuberance, he felt a universal benevolence and kinship with all mankind. He was delighted to see anyone.

But the person he hailed recognized him first, and

came to a dead halt in the roadway, waiting for him to approach. It was Lilith, and her face was pale with suffering.

Instantly, concern erased his cheeriness. "Lilith," he said in alarm, once he was close enough to see her face. "What's wrong? What's happened?" He came up to her and put his hand on her shoulder. She stared at him and did not pull away. "Lilith. Are you all right?"

"You're alive," she said.

He laughed, but kindly, because she looked so wretched. "Yes, of course I'm alive. I'm sorry—were you anxious about me? I didn't think—"

Suddenly she wrenched away from him. Her hands had flown to her cheeks; she looked at him over the barrier of her fingers. "You have been gone five days," she said flatly. "I thought you were dead."

"I'm sorry," he said quietly. "I didn't realize you would worry. You have never worried about me before."

"I thought you were dead," she said again. And it was then he realized that she was weeping—silently, hopelessly—surely for the first time.

He took one quick step forward and swept her into his arms. For a moment he was conscious of the awkward, angled arrangement of her bones, and then she relaxed into his embrace. She seemed actually to melt into flesh and blood as her body leaned against his, as if she learned the textures and the substances from him. He felt her shoulders shake, and he felt her terrific tension as she tried to repress her sobs. He stroked her hair soothingly; he whispered wordless endearments and repeated his apology countless times. Yet a traitorous elation crept through him. She wept, and she wept for him.

Abruptly she pulled back, not quite escaping the enclosure of his arms. Her expression was, at the same time, vulnerable and defensive. "You were gone five days," she repeated. "I thought you would not come back."

He freed one hand to brush the hair from her forehead. And the unbelievable wetness of tears along her cheeks—he had to touch that, too. "Haven't I told you that I will not leave you?" he murmured. "And didn't you believe me?"

"What were you doing?"

He laughed softly. "You wouldn't believe me if I told you."

"What, though?"

"Learning to love you better."

She shook her hand in automatic denial, but a faint, self-conscious flush rose to her cheeks. He laughed again. "I didn't think it was possible," he added, and drew her close again.

He bent his head to kiss her, for the second time in his life—a real kiss this time, full on her mouth. She was tentative and shy as a girl who had never been kissed, but she seemed to like it; her mouth was pliant under his, willing to experiment. As he kissed her lips, they seemed to grow fuller, richer, more plush. Heat rose under her cool skin, almost vein by vein. She spoke a muffled phrase and pressed her body closer. Her hands were locked together behind his back.

And then suddenly, she flung herself from him again, more violently this time. The force of her resistance pushed Aubrey back three steps and actually brought her to her knees.

"Lilith," he began, starting forward, but she jumped up and backed away from him. He froze.

If she had been wretched before, she was wild now. "Oh, what have you done to me?" she cried.

"What have I *done* to you?" he exclaimed. "What have *I* done—"

"You have made my life intolerable!"

"Lilith!"

Kneading her hands on the front of her gray dress, she began to pace. "He changed my shape, but he didn't change *me*," she said over her shoulder. "Nothing touched me, nothing moved me; I did not care for Glyrenden or for any man. I looked like a woman, but I was what I had always been. He could not make me feel as human beings do.

"But you—from the beginning, it was different with you. At first I thought it was just a matter of *like* or *dislike*—mild words, mild emotions. I thought you just made my life more pleasant—and I had certainly come to learn the difference between pleasant and unpleasant in my three years with Glyrenden. I don't know how it happened that you became important to me. I don't know when it began to please me to know that you cared for me. Or when it began to matter if you were alive or dead."

"I am glad that it matters," he interposed quickly.

"Well, I am not glad!" she retorted. "How can I live as Glyrenden's wife—how can I stand to have him touch me again, now—now that I have learned to feel?"

The sense of her words struck him like a blow; he saw precisely how he had betrayed her. He started to speak, failed, and tried again. "I did not mean—it was not my intention—to hurt you," he said, stammering a little. "I was in love with you before I knew what you are. It is human nature to try and win affection from the creature that one loves. I did not mean to change you to do so."

She had stopped pacing. Now she stood still, staring down at the thick carpet of pine needles beneath her feet. Her face had grown dull and homely again; he was not sure she was listening to him. "Once the transformation starts, it cannot be stopped," she said. "If I learn to love like a woman, I learn all the other things women know—hate and fear and passion, boredom and jealousy and all the rest. I become like all those other women."

"Never like them," Aubrey interjected.

"And I slowly lose the things I knew before," she went on, still ignoring him. "I mistake the turning of the seasons. I can no longer understand the language of the wind. I cannot remember what it was like to stand naked under the winter moonlight and be coldly beautiful."

"But I love you," Aubrey said. "What can I give you that will make up for those other things?"

She shook her head; she would not look at him. "I do not want the things you have to give me," she said. "I do not want to be changed, either by magic or by love."

"But you have been changed," he whispered. "What will you do now?"

The intensity of his voice caught her attention. She finally looked over at him, and what she saw in his eyes made her back away a step. "I will do what I have always done," she said. "I will wait for him to release me."

"But he won't! And it will kill you to live with him!"

"What choice do I have?"

He bounded forward, catching her hands before she could retreat again. "Come away with me," he pleaded. "Leave with me today—now. There is nothing I need back at Glyrenden's house—"

She was shaking her head. She was twisting her fingers against his hold, but she could not free herself. "Aubrey, no—he will look for us—"

"We can be in the next kingdom in three days' time. Within a few weeks, we can be so far from here, he will never find us. I am not so ill a magician—I can disguise all traces of our passage—"

Her face had become obdurate; she made her trapped hands into fists. "I will not go away with you. I cannot leave him."

"Why?" he demanded. "Why?"

"You can only change me more," she said. "You cannot change me back. You cannot give me what I want."

He almost flung her hands back at her; she staggered a little before regaining her balance. "He will not give you what you want either!" Aubrey cried. "Would you rather be a miserable woman with Glyrenden or a contented one with me?"

Stubbornly she shook her head. "Hope was the first human emotion I learned," she said. "With him, I have hope. With you, I have only love. It is not enough."

He closed his eyes. He was suddenly exhausted. "I have love, but no hope," he said. "I cannot tell which is worse."

She came close enough to touch him, and he opened his eyes again to look down at her. On her face was a small, timid smile. "Please," she said. "I do not want to fight with you. I do not want to be angry with you—or you with me. Let us—let us be the way we were."

She did not know how to express regret or fear; she did not even know that she was afraid of losing him. Aubrey watched her, wondering what else she would learn, without knowing it, against her will. "Do you want me to stay, then?" he asked slowly. "If I can only make your life worse, I will go now."

"No," she said quickly. "You make it more difficult, but you do not make it worse. I don't—I am not sure how I would survive now without you."

"I cannot stop loving you," he warned. "If that prohibition is to be a condition of my staying on, I will have to go."

The color rose again in her face, but she shook her head. "I will not try to change you if you do not try to change me," she said. "Please stay."

He wanted to kiss her again, or at least kiss her hand, but instead he gave her a short, courtly bow. "I will," he said. Clasping her fingers in his, he led her back to the road; and hand-in-hand they began the long walk back to Glyrenden's house. But Aubrey thought they had both lied not so long ago, though neither would admit it. He knew what it was to hope, and she knew what it was to love.

Glyrenden was home when they returned, but he did not seem to notice that his wife and his apprentice had been gone. He sat in the kitchen, on one of the sturdy wooden chairs, with Eve perched tremulously on the chair beside him. Orion, seated on the far side of the room, watched them both with his usual apprehensive attention. Arachne, moving from table to countertop as she prepared the evening meal, cast them frequent furtive glances and whispered animadversions as she worked.

Glyrenden had eyes for no one but Eve. "Ah, my beauty," he gloated, stroking her soft hair. "How I missed you while I was gone! How I wished you could have come with me. You are not ready yet for the company of great men, but soon. Soon, you will travel with me wherever I go."

Eve stared up at him with her huge brown eyes, despair and supplication mixed upon her face. She shivered under his hands, and said nothing.

Aubrey stood on the threshold so long that Lilith brushed past him to enter. She took her customary seat at the table, glanced at her husband and glanced away. She did not look again at Aubrey.

And Aubrey continued to stand at the door, incapable of moving forward, incapable of walking out of the room. *How much longer can I endure this?* he was thinking. *And what can I do?*

Glyrenden had only been home for two days—during which time almost no one spoke, almost no one ate, and almost no one seemed to breathe—when a messenger came to the front door looking for him. They were all still at the breakfast table when they were summoned by the broken music of the mistuned bells.

Glyrenden was spooning honey-sweetened cereal into Eve's mouth, and he scowled at the unexpected interruption. "Who could be calling here?" he demanded. "I am not expecting visitors."

Aubrey was glad enough of an excuse to leave the room. "Shall I go see?" he offered, already on his feet. Glyrenden waved his assent.

Aubrey hastened down the dusty hall, wrestled open the heavy door and stared in displeasure at the figure of Royel Stephanis.

"Her husband is here," was Aubrey's curt greeting. "You had best be on your way immediately."

As before, the young lord slipped inside the doorway before Aubrey had time to stop him. "It is Glyrenden I am here for," Royel said. "I have been sent by the king to fetch him back to court."

Aubrey had forgotten that Royel had been appointed to serve his liege. But even so. "I am surprised that the king would treat a nobleman as a messenger or page," he said.

"I volunteered to come," Royel said. "Now, will you take me to him?"

So Aubrey led the young lord back through the hallway, past the rusty suit of armor and the cracked stone stairway, into the kitchen, where the rest of the household waited. He wondered what Royel would make of this scene—the wizard's wife sitting calmly at the table while her husband hovered possessively over a beautiful, frightened young girl. *If anything was needed to convince Royel that Lilith should trust his love*, thought Aubrey in resignation, *this particular glimpse of domesticity should do it.*

"Royel Stephanis, with a message from the king," Aubrey announced, stepping into the kitchen with Royel at his heels. Glyrenden dropped his spoon and whipped around, but no one else in the room seemed much interested. Eve took advantage of Glyrenden's distraction to pull her chair as far back from his as possible. Lilith sipped at her milk and glanced at the figure in the doorway. Arachne and Orion paid him no attention at all.

"A message from the king?" Glyrenden snapped, coming to his feet. "I left him a few days ago, and he said he would not need me for another two weeks."

"A matter of some urgency has arisen," Royel said stiffly. He covered it well, but Aubrey suspected he was rigid with shock. By a supreme effort of will, the boy kept his eyes fixed on Glyrenden and did not once look in Lilith's direction. "I have a parchment here, closed with his seal."

"Let me have it," Glyrenden said, and snatched it from Royel's outstretched hand.

What he read there apparently satisfied him—even pleased him—for he laughed shortly and folded the paper twice. "I will be with you in ten minutes," he said. "There are sorcerous objects I must collect."

The wizard left the room. Royel's eyes went instantly to Lilith's face. "I have wondered—I wanted to know—I wished to know you were well," the young man stammered, though he had spoken with great coolness to the mage. "I was glad for a chance to come here—to see you again, however briefly—"

"I am fine," Lilith replied. She met his eyes fleetingly and looked away.

"Coffee? A meal?" Aubrey asked practically. "You must have ridden all night."

"I broke my journey late last evening in a village nearby," Royel said. "I did not want to arrive in the middle of the night."

"Well, you may as well eat something while you're here," Aubrey said, and pushed him toward the table.

But Royel, like everyone else in that house, had no appetite. He took a chair close to Lilith's and spoke to her in a low, intense voice. "You seem unwell—unhappy," he said. "How can I aid you? Who is that girl?"

Lilith glanced at Eve. "My husband's niece," she said.

"His niece!"

"Royel—" Aubrey said warningly.

Royel turned disbelieving eyes in his direction. "She is not that man's niece!" he exclaimed.

"It is better for all concerned if we say so," Aubrey said. "Eat, and prepare yourself for a long ride back to court in the magician's company."

Instead, Royel edged even closer to the wizard's wife and took her hand in his. She regarded him steadily, with no expression. "If I return for you," the young man said, "would you come away with me? I could take you to safety, I could take you to freedom—"

"No," she replied.

"But I love you!"

She pulled her hand away and picked up her glass of milk. Glyrenden stepped through the hallway door, back into the kitchen.

"Ah, I see that my charming wife has fed you," the wizard said gaily. It was impossible to tell what he had seen, overheard or suspected. "Come, young Stephanis. The king's message was sent in some agitation. We have no time to waste."

Royel came reluctantly to his feet and bowed impartially to all those in the room. "The saints willing, I will see you again shortly," he said.

Glyrenden laughed. "Oh, I am sure you will become intimate with all of us," he said. "In time."

The wizard bent to kiss Lilith on the mouth. When he lifted his head, he kept his fingers cupped under her chin for a moment. "Once again I am reminded how beautiful you are," he murmured. "Do not forget, I will be back quite soon."

Next, he took Eve in a close embrace, drawing her up from her chair to hold her small, shaking body against his chest. "My dearest," he murmured into her dark hair. "The next time, I swear it, you shall travel with me."

These farewells made, the wizard turned to laugh at

the young lord, who stood waiting with his face utterly immobile. "Shall we be on our way?" he suggested, and led the boy out of the room. Royel risked one last, hopeless glance back at Lilith. In a few moments, the noise of their passage died away, and they were gone.

"There goes a very foolish young man," Aubrey said severely.

"And a very cruel old one," Lilith responded.

Thirteen

FOUR DAYS LATER, GLYRENDEN RETURNED. HE WAS RIDing his bad-tempered black stallion and leading a horse that looked very much like the one Royel had ridden in on. Behind them, running as though his legs were aching and his muscles unused to so much work, pattered a mixed-breed hound just past puppyhood. As the small cavalcade reached the doorway of the wizard's house, the dog collapsed to its belly with an audible sigh, closed its eyes and was instantly asleep.

Lilith and Aubrey, just back from their afternoon stroll, turned silently to observe the new arrivals. Eve, who had been sitting on the ground before the flower garden, came to her feet uncertainly as the wizard dismounted. The horses backed nervously away from Glyrenden's hands, creating so much disturbance that, in the end, Aubrey came forward to take the reins of both animals. He secured them to the hitching post and untied Glyrenden's saddlebags from the stallion's back.

Then he turned and stared down at the hound now sleeping at the door.

"Was this not an odd thing?" Glyrenden said, although no one had questioned him at all. "We were not halfway to the palace when a rattlesnake uncoiled from the ground at our feet, and this excitable steed reared to

180

the air and threw his master. Young Stephanis was killed
instantly, though I did my best to save him. When I took
the sad news to the king, he expressed great grief and
thanked me for my attempts to succor him. In reward, he
gave me the boy's own mount, and his favorite hound as
well. I like the dog, but the horse is something of a
brute. If I cannot tame it, it will have to be gotten rid
of."

Now Orion and Arachne had emerged from the house,
drawn by the nervous nicker of the horses or some even
stronger portent of disaster. Orion had gone to the
beasts' heads and miraculously calmed both; Arachne
had come to a halt before the dog and looked down on it
with a heavy frown. *Hair to clean up from all the furniture and who knows if it's housebroken?* she might have
been thinking, from the expression on her face. In her
hand she carried a long-bladed kitchen knife, for she had
evidently been interrupted while preparing the evening
meal, and this she wiped mindlessly on the dirty hem of
her apron. Eve had made herself into a small, shivering
pile on the front porch. Lilith, unmoved as ever, merely
watched Aubrey.

Aubrey stood with his head bowed and horror moving
through his veins like acid. He could not have said why
this was worse, but it was. It was so bad it could not be
lived with. The decision that he could not make had suddenly been made for him.

"Turn him back," he said to Glyrenden without even
lifting his head.

Glyrenden had been sorting through his saddlebags
for something acquired at court, and when he brought
his gaze around to Aubrey he looked blank and preoccu-
pied for a minute. "I beg your pardon?" he said.

Aubrey raised his eyes, looked levelly at Glyrenden, and said a little more loudly, "Turn him back."

The wizard dropped his bags and straightened, to return Aubrey's steady stare with an unfriendly one of his own. "I don't know what you're talking about."

Aubrey pointed. "The dog. That was once a man. And the king's man, at that. Turn him back."

For a moment, Aubrey thought the wizard would deny it again, but then suddenly the older man laughed. The sound cut a discordant swath across the cheerful colors of the autumn afternoon. "He amuses me as he is."

"Turn him back anyway."

"At your command? I think not."

"Turn him back. Or I will transform him myself."

Glyrenden seemed to grow thinner and tauter, and his black eyes resembled the night sky, so full were they of distant points of cold light. "You will have to kill me to be able to counteract my spells."

"Yes," said Aubrey. "Turn him back, or I will do it myself."

They were standing in the small clearing before the house, hedged in on all sides by trees and overgrown shrubbery and the house itself. As Aubrey spoke, the space seemed to shrink down by half, as if all things living within a mile of that arena drew closer to watch. Eve stopped shivering, the hound lifted its head; but neither of the antagonists noticed. They had attention for nothing except each other.

"You are good," Glyrenden murmured, "but are you that good? I have not taught you all I know."

"But I have learned much without your help," Aubrey said calmly. Now that the moment had come, the cancer in his stomach had melted away; now he would kill Glyrenden or be killed. Either way, he would no longer have to live cozily with guilty knowledge, and relief made his mind exultant and finely honed.

Glyrenden spat out a single syllable of contempt. "I do not fear what others have taught you," he said.

"It is not their education I intend to put to use," Aubrey replied.

"Well, then," Glyrenden said, and not another word. Almost before Aubrey realized Glyrenden had picked up the gauntlet, the battle was joined. Glyrenden was suddenly no longer a thin, restless man; he was a huge, wide-jawed wolf midway through a deadly lunge for Aubrey's throat.

But neither was Aubrey any longer a man. He had become a hawk, and his wings beat the air a full two feet above the head of the snarling predator. Then Aubrey dove, his talons curved to hook into his enemy's black eyes. But the wolf had flattened to the ground, and was a cougar, and sprang up again with a yowl, to leap for the banking hawk. Aubrey felt the thinnest imaginable scimitar of the cat's claw catch in the tip of his left wing, and on the instant, he was changed. He was a bear, bigger than Orion, with paws as huge as skillets, and he swiped at the cougar's squalling face with every nail extended.

But the cougar was gone. In its place was a rock, colorless and flinty, impervious to teeth and claws. Aubrey fell on it from above in the shape of a metal spike, six feet long and viciously pointed at the tip. A jagged line cracked down the stone's rough surface; then the two combatants both fell to the ground. Briefly they were men again, themselves, one dark and one fair. They rolled to their feet with four yards between them and measured each other with human eyes.

"So," Glyrenden said, "you have been practicing while I was away."

"Cyril must have told you how quickly I learn."

"He told me. I confess I did not believe him."

"Have you never met any wizard more skilled than you?"

"Oh, Cyril is a better illusionist, and better at calling up visions in water or glass. And there are others with talents I cannot quite match. But in this—no, my pet, I have never met my equal."

"Turn him back," Aubrey said again. "Turn them all back."

Glyrenden merely smiled. His smile was so wide that his face became all teeth, his whole body a grinning face; he had grown monstrous, he was a dragon, his skin the rusty color of autumn trees and his fearsome teeth whiter than milk. The dragon growled deep in its throat and reared back, then fell forward with the power of falling rock to land in a heap upon the other wizard and crush him.

But Aubrey was too small and too agile; he had become a fly, tiny and inconsequential, riding on the dragon's back. Dragon no more; Glyrenden melted before him to a limpid pool of water, thrashing itself into a rough sea that would drown the insect resting precariously on its surface. But the insect dashed to safe ground and grew ferociously, bursting into flame at the edge of the stormy lake. The water rose, spilling its imaginary banks to drown the blaze, but the fire was far stronger; its heat drove back every watcher in the woods.

Like dew under summer sunlight, the pool evaporated, but much more quickly; Glyrenden hovered over Aubrey as mist in the air. The fire suddenly vanished and in its place was a devastating chill, pursuing the heavy cloud of moisture that was the wizard. Glyrenden fell to the ground in a long white line of frost, diamond-backed; the crystals coalesced, and he was a snake, copper-colored and hissing. Aubrey chopped at his head as a descending axe, but the snake had become rust and clung to the iron of the blade. Aubrey changed to glass, fragile and slippery; Glyrenden shattered him as a bullet, catapulted from nowhere. But the glass was now sand, inches deep and unresisting. It smothered the cartridge with its weight.

Metamorphosis: The bullet writhed once and became a weed, able to grow in any soil, poking its shaggy head above the ridgeline of the dune. Then a great wind arose, focused and precise, whipping up the atoms of the sand to animal height, chest height, man height; then it was Aubrey again, on his feet but stooping over to snap the weed off its stalk.

But in his hand the weed changed to a bramble, thick with thorns; blood dotted Aubrey's palm in half-a-dozen places. He cursed softly, with an odd impatience, but kept his hold on the briar. The air was so still that his murmured words should have carried to all corners of the forest, but he spoke so quietly that no one understood what he said.

And then standing before him, dazed and uncertain, stood Glyrenden, who had been changed by someone else's magic from one form to another. Just an instant he stood there, fury and comprehension coming to him together, but Aubrey did not wait for his wits to regather. He snatched the kitchen knife from Arachne's hands and dove for the black-haired wizard, and he drove the entire length of the blade deep into Glyrenden's heart. There was a moment when everything in the world was utterly motionless. Then, in a slow, elegant pirouette, Glyrenden fell to the ground at Aubrey's feet.

Then it was as if every beast in the forest let loose at

once with whatever howl, cry or moan its throat would carry; there was a cacophony of primitive elation that rose from all sides, miles in each direction. Trees cavorted from the force of a driving wind, or created the wind themselves, whipping their branches from side to side till they clattered and interlaced. Behind Aubrey, slowly, as if stone by stone were being pried loose and dropped, the sloppy gray mansion that was Glyrenden's house toppled to the ground and began to disintegrate.

In the clearing just in front of the decomposing porch, the five living creatures that remained tried to keep their balance on suddenly shifting ground and strained to recover their numbed and disordered senses.

Aubrey woke from what seemed like a trance to find himself still clutching the bloodied knife and staring down at the crumpled figure of the dead wizard. It was a frightening thing to watch. Glyrenden had been dead less than a minute, yet all the scavengers of the forest had already gone savagely to work on him, the ants, the maggots, the fungi and the molds. Across each wrist and ankle, and wound around the white throat, creepers twined to bind him in place. His sooty black hair had fallen back from his white face, and the shape and structure of the skull could be plainly seen under the besieged membrane of the skin. By nightfall, not a bone nor scrap of hair would be left; not a rock would mark the place the house had stood. Glyrenden and his effects would have disappeared.

Aubrey roused himself with a sudden fear, and before he even looked to check who still attended him, he raised his arms and spoke a quick spell of suspension. All movement halted within the radius of his incantation; the trees stopped their swaying, the busy ants froze, the grass lay quiet again. The bear, which had staggered to its hind feet, slumped down on its haunches. The tiny brown spider, scuttling toward the promising overhang of a felled gray brick, stopped in her sticky tracks. The young man lying on his side, horror and bewilderment on his face, settled in to sleep again. The fawn froze with one foot curled against her chest.

But Lilith had not moved at all, and she only stirred now when Aubrey came over to her.

"He's dead," Aubrey said to her unnecessarily.

She nodded. "For how long have you meant to kill him?" she asked.

"I suppose ever since I realized what he had done, and that he would not undo it."

She gestured toward the others. "You have freed them with his death. Is that what you thought would happen?"

"Most of a wizard's magics die with him. They tell stories of rubies turning to rocks and whole mountain ranges melting back into meadows when the death of the great sorcerer Talvis finally reversed some of his spells. But a good wizard can make magic that lasts after his death. He can speak spells that are so true they become the truth, and then only new magic can reverse them again."

Now she looked at him, and plainly in the green eyes he saw the unspeakable longing he had only sensed before. Very simply, she said, "Can you change me?"

"I think so," he said, "but I am not sure."

She glanced at the body of Glyrenden, then back at Aubrey. "You changed him against his will in the heat of battle. I would think that would be a harder thing."

Aubrey smiled with no mirth whatsoever. "My old teacher, Cyril, always told me it was easier to kill than to create," he said. "I never understood what he meant, but the only spells he taught me were spells of creation, and they were very hard indeed. By comparison, destruction is much simpler. I have learned that for the first time today."

"I don't understand," she said.

Aubrey pointed to a pile of fallen stones and they both sat. He carefully refrained from touching her. "To change something from one form to another is a difficult task, and the spells to do so are among the hardest things I have ever learned. To change a thing that has been made something else by magic is even harder, and the risks are greater. It was possible that I would kill Glyrenden by changing him back to his true form, but since I planned to kill him anyway, I did not greatly care. I run the same risk if I try to change you."

"Oh," she said.

"But I will try if you want me to."

"Yes," she said. "I want you to."

Aubrey made no reply to that, hoping she might add a word or two to soften the finality of her choice, but she said nothing else. Finally, he rose to his feet again and made his way to where the other creatures waited, stayed in place by his quickly woven command.

He placed his hand over the bear's eyes and took from him all knowledge of what it meant to be a man. He took away the memory of table and bedroom, village and fair, the rudiments of speech and the taste of cooked meat. He took away the hatred of mankind that he found in Orion's heart, but he left the sense of terror that even a man's faint scent could bring. "Go now," he whispered, releasing the bear from the spell that held him in place. "Live well and happily, and avoid humankind for the rest of your days."

He knelt beside the small brown spider and laid a finger fleetingly on her hunched back. There was little room in that tiny brain for memory, but Aubrey cleaned those cluttered cells as best he could of the shape and re- membrance of womanhood. In her true form, she was a dainty thing, no beauty but delicately made. Aubrey stroked her back with the gentlest of motions. "Forget everything," he murmured to her, "except your fear of men." Then he lifted his hand and she hurried away, moving as fast as her thin, fine legs would carry her.

The fawn watched him motionlessly, her great eyes at their widest, and even under the spell of stillness, she trembled. Aubrey put his palms to either side of her pointed face and closed her eyes with his thumbs; and as he closed her eyes he wiped away all the interior images that caused her still to shiver. Almost immediately, she quieted, and almost as quickly grew frantic again. For he had not taken from her that instinctive distrust of man, and here he was, a man and holding her. He let his hands drop away and he undid his spell, and she darted away through the welcoming forest without a backward glance.

Last, Aubrey turned to the sleeping man, little more than a boy and wearing, even as he dreamed, a puzzled, frightened look. Aubrey rested his hand upon Royel's brow and pulled from his thoughts all memory of the past four days, the journey to Glyrenden's house, the aw- ful moment of transfiguration itself, the feel of the dog's feet, the foreign smoothness of the beast's muscles, the sound of the hound's baying, so strangely liquid coming from one's own throat. He hesitated as he rummaged through Royel's mind and found image after image of Lilith, but in the end, he allowed the boy to keep those visions. Had positions been reversed, he would not have wanted Royel to destroy his own pictures of the wizard's wife; he could be that generous in return.

To replace the memories he took away, Aubrey fashioned new ones, of a fall from his horse, a dizzy day of amnesia, and two days of being nursed to health by a friendly peasant woman. The king might wonder why Glyrenden's version of the young lord's disappearance differed so radically from Royel's own, but he would soon have more to wonder about as Glyrenden's disappearance raised more questions. *And those questions*, Aubrey thought, will *never be answered*.

He rose to his feet and glanced over at Lilith, who watched him still. The boy at his feet continued to sleep. "Is he dead?" Lilith wanted to know.

"No," Aubrey said. "But I think it will be best if we are gone from here before he wakes up. I am not eager to answer any questions he may have."

She glanced around the clearing, which was less of a clearing every moment that they stayed. Aubrey had lifted his spell of suspension, and the forest was creeping closer, almost as they stood there and watched. "He may find this a strange place to awake if he sleeps too long."

"I have laid a protection upon him. He will not be harmed."

"And what news of Glyrenden will he carry back to the king?"

"No news, but only the rumor that will soon be on everyone's lips—the great wizard is dead."

She looked at the body of her slain husband with no expression on her face. "There will be no proof of that."

"No," said Aubrey. "But he is still dead."

She came to her feet and looked at him directly, and he marveled again at how green her eyes were, such beautiful eyes in such a plain and such a beloved face. "And me?" she asked.

"We will walk to the King's Grove," Aubrey said, "which is a place I have long wanted to see. And then I will leave, and you will stay, and the world will be as it was before Glyrenden was ever born."

"Not quite the same," she whispered, and for a moment he thought he saw the faintest glitter of tears in her eyes. "For you will remember and use the spells he taught you. And I—I will live a long time with an alien memory in my heart."

Aubrey was silent a moment. "No," he said at last, very slowly. "You will be as you once were, with no thought except what belongs to you, and no memory except that of soil and season. I have made the others forget, and I will make you forget, and these three years will be as if they never were."

"But if I am made to forget Glyrenden," she said, still whispering, "does that mean I will forget you as well?"

"Yes," he said.

"Then I do not want to forget."

He was silent, for a wild hope laid a strangulating hand across his throat, and speech was impossible. She had felt nothing at all for Glyrenden, not love and not hate, for she was fashioned of a living thing that had no passions, desires or emotions. But she had been three years a woman, treated as a woman and loved as a woman by three very different men; she had speech and reason and a soul. Perhaps the transformation she had feared so greatly had finally come to pass.

"Lilith," he said at last, his voice very low. "I know what you have suffered at Glyrenden's hands and that you could never have come to love the man he was. But I am not like Glyrenden, and I have loved you for a long time. I will do what you say—I will take you where you want to go. But my life will be sere and empty without you. The world that once seemed so full of color and promise will be gray and tedious. Say you will stay with me. Remain a woman and become my wife. You do not know how good that life can be. I swear I would die to make you happy."

She was silent a moment, her head bowed, her marvelous eyes hidden. Then she lifted her head and he could see she was crying, even though she smiled. She came closer and put her two hands on either side of his face; and it was the first time he could remember that she had reached out to him. "It would not make me happy for you to die," she said. "And if I could be happy as a woman, I know it would be at your side. But you forget so many things, Aubrey, my dear. You forget how strange I am, and that even simple peasants recognize that strangeness in me—"

"They would say nothing against you while I was near," he interrupted swiftly.

"You forget that I have no family, that I cannot make friends, that I have no skills and no conversation. I could not move with you in the world of men, in the exalted circles in which you will someday move."

"I do not care for the society of rich and exalted men. I would be content in a cottage in an untracked forest, if you were in the cottage with me."

She smiled again. "You would not be content. You are a great wizard, Aubrey, and you are destined to be with great men. It would not help you to have me at your side."

"I love you," he said helplessly. "It could not hurt me to have you near me for the rest of my life."

"But Aubrey," she said, "can you not see how it will hurt me?"

"But then do you not care for me at all?" he cried desperately. "I thought—it seemed—surely you feel some affection for me after all?"

"I think I must love you," she said, her voice very low. "For I feel as if this parting will break my heart. And I did not think I had a heart."

He flung himself to the ground at her feet. "Then stay with me," he begged. "A little while, stay with me. See what it is like to be a woman in love with a man. After that little while, I will ask you again, and then whatever you decide I will do."

She looked down at him unflinchingly. "And then you will beg me again to stay just a little while, and again, and again, and soon I will forget to be anything except a woman and I will even be happy that that is what I am. But Aubrey, that is not what I want to be. I have been twisted out of my purpose, turned by black enchantment from my true shape, and I have been unhappier than you can imagine for three interminable years. There is a willow missing from the King's Grove where I was supposed to stand and make the forest complete. The world is out of kilter, just a little, because I am not where I should be. And I want to be there, Aubrey. I love you, but I do not love you enough."

He dropped his head, and his shoulders seemed to draw in against his neck and make his whole body smaller. For a moment more he knelt before her, no longer pleading, but unable to climb again to his feet. She watched him, but did not touch him or speak again. At last, he looked up, then stood again, and on his face was the forlorn look of a man for whom all magic has faded.

"Let us go then to the King's Grove," he said, and his voice, though soft, was steady. "We can forage for our food. There is nothing here either of us needs to pack or carry. Let us walk to the King's Grove."

She could not help herself; she put one hand on his arm and the other to his cheek again. "But let us make the trip slowly," she said, "so it takes us at least three days."

It took them four days to make the journey to the King's Grove. Those four days, Aubrey knew, would be the last happy days of his life, and the only happy days Lilith had known in her three years as a woman. Aubrey hoped, though he did not voice his hope, that those four days would make her reconsider her decision, for during that time she loved him as much as any woman had ever loved him. But on the morning of the fifth day, they eluded the armed sentinels patrolling the borders of the King's Grove, and he knew that Lilith had not for an instant wavered in her determination.

For as soon as they stepped onto that protected soil, into that perfect and sanctified garden, she fell away from him. Her hand dropped from his arm, her body seemed to change and roughen; all her attention, which had been fixed on him, focused elsewhere. She ran from oak to elm to cedar with a childish delight, touching one coarse trunk, then another, naming to herself their real names, the names by which they addressed each other. The wind had picked up and danced through the bare autumn branches with an excited motion. They had no speech men could understand, these trees, but Aubrey almost thought he heard the fantastic, ancient language of the dryads as the news flew instantly from one end of the sacred grove to the other: *She's back, she's back, the one long gone has returned to us at last.*

And when the woman finally rejoined him, and took his hand impatiently to draw him to the right spot, the special place, the oddly bare patch of land that was the one corner of the earth set aside for her particular use, he knew none of the last-minute supplications he had prepared would sway her. For she had changed already; it was a stranger's impersonal hand she laid in his, and her fey green eyes held virtually no recognition as they met his. He almost thought he could leave her in this place, still in the body of a woman, and the very intensity of her longing would gradually turn her back to the thing she once was. That greatly had she altered during the few short minutes they had stood inside this grove.

But speech was still left to her, though even with that she was impatient, using as few words as possible to convey her meaning. "Here," she demanded. "Now. This place." She planted her feet and with a luxurious, sensuous motion, spread her arms as wide as they would go.

He used his sternest voice, trying to catch her remote attention. "Lilith. Remember what I told you before. This is a hard spell, the hardest, and it is possible I could kill you instead of change you. You realize that, don't you? You still want me to speak the incantation?"

"Yes, yes," she said, flinging her head back and closing her incredible eyes. "Now. Say it now."

And he gazed once more at the coiled braids around her head and the simple, elegant lines of her body, and knew a craven moment of rebellion. If he did not speak the spell, she would never be changed; not a wizard in this kingdom could reverse Glyrenden's magic except himself. She would still be a woman. She would follow him wherever he went, needing something from him she could get nowhere else. She would be with him always, for he would never change her. He loved her. She would be his forever.

But he knew, even in that split second while the evil thought took hold of him, that he would never hold her so against her will. That would make him no better than Glyrenden; that was one thing. For another, he loved the woman known as Lilith, and he would not be able to live with her unhappiness. So he closed his eyes, so he would not have to watch her while he spoke this spell, and silently he chanted the charm that would change a woman to a willow. And he put into the enchantment all the baffles he knew, all the protectors, all the safeguards. He made the spell so strong not even Glyrenden, had he been alive, would have been able to undo it.

And then he opened his eyes. It was the most beautiful, the most awful thing he had ever seen, this transformation of a woman to a tree. Her body thickened and grew brown, her legs lengthened and rooted slowly in the earth. Her arms stretched and her fingers stretched, and tiny twigs began forming on her fingertips. He had missed the point where her brown head melted into the silver-brown trunk, for suddenly her face was no longer to be seen, and then none of her body was to be seen, and her slim, wiry branches arched over him like a rainfall, splashing in all directions. It was nearly winter, but she dazzled him with a repertoire of seasons; hard buds formed on her long, delicate limbs, then unfurled to a brief, heady green, then crinkled up and became old, and fell lazily around his feet. The trailing, clinging branches closed about him, brushing his shoulders and chest, and he had to push them aside with some force to move away from her, out from under her shade and into the white sunlight.

She had told him she wanted to remember and so he let her remember, but he did not think it would take any spell of his to make her forget. As for himself, no magician in the world would be able to take this memory from his mind; it had patterned itself over the intricate whorls and ridges of his brain and would be a part of him till the day he died. He stood looking for one long moment at the single willow in the King's Grove, which was more beautiful than any object he had ever seen; then he stooped to retrieve something that had fallen from her when she changed. It was the gold necklace he had given her, which she had worn for the past four days and had no use for now. Aubrey pocketed it and turned away, and made his way as quickly as he could back past the guards and out of the grove of trees.

Epilogue

SOME SAY THAT IS THE END OF THE STORY, AND SOME SAY it is not. For while much is known of Aubrey's life, he who became known as the Gifted, much still lies within the realm of myth and speculation. Some say he never again laid eyes on the woman known as Lilith and that she remained as he had changed her until the king's forest burned down and all life within it perished. Others say that is not so.

These eager romantics will tell you that, as the forest took fire, and one by one the trees succumbed, spicy cedar lending its burning fragrance to the hot pitch of the pine, one tree did not burn when the flames reached it. That tree shook in the acrid breath of the approaching fire, and collapsed in upon itself, and remembered, when the need was upon it to remember, how to be a woman and how to run. And that woman escaped the conflagration that destroyed every other living thing in the King's Grove; and she stole clothes from the first peasant's hut she came to, unwatched and untended; and she made her way slowly from village to village, stealing food and remembering the language, until she reached a town that was large enough to have news. They say that there she inquired as to the whereabouts of a wizard named Aubrey, and that she traveled to the place where he lived, which was a thousand miles and two kingdoms from the grove where she had started. And that they were reunited that one time and never again, for they were never again parted from that day until the day they died.

It is true, as these storytellers say, that the King's Grove burned down; and it is true that in his later years, Aubrey the Gifted had with him at all times a woman companion who was reputed to be green-eyed and strange. Any record of the magician's life will give you these facts. But as to the woman's identity, there are no clues. None of the histories record her name, and it is hard to believe that a spell spoken by Aubrey the Gifted could be so easily overturned. Moreover, she had once preferred the risk of death to the prospect of life as a woman, and she had had many years to forget that she had once had feet and could run from the threatened fire. But the stories persist, and no scholar has definitely refuted them.

As for the great magician, Glyrenden, the stories are even stranger. It is said that you can spend your whole life quartering the king's domain and never yet come across the wizard's remains. That whole forested area, to this day still wild and nearly impenetrable, is so overgrown that it is impossible to find in it any of the paths and roadways that once existed. The forest has taken its revenge on Glyrenden, the villagers say, and obliterated all traces of his existence, so that even those who have heard about him from others who have heard about him cannot prove he ever once lived and breathed and cast malicious spells; and they cannot be inspired to emulate a man who has disappeared so entirely from the memory of the earth.